The Silent Matter

STORIES

Suchhanda Chatterjee

Om Books International

First published in 2024 by

Om Books International

Corporate & Editorial Office
A-12, Sector 64, Noida 201 301
Uttar Pradesh, India
Phone: +91 120 477 4100
Email: editorial@ombooks.com
Website: www.ombooksinternational.com

Sales Office
107, Ansari Road, Darya Ganj,
New Delhi 110 002, India
Phone: +91 11 4000 9000
Email: sales@ombooks.com
Website: www.ombooks.com

ISBN: 978-93-6395-825-8

Printed in India

10 9 8 7 6 5 4 3 2 1

Suchhanda 'Meenoo' Chatterjee is a producer, storyteller and founder of Quest Films and Ishtaa Films. She has been writing from the age of eighteen. She served as the creative producer for *Forbidden Love* (Zee5), an anthology of romantic thrillers, in which two of her stories, *Arranged Marriage* and *Anamika*, were directed by Pradeep Sarkar and Priyadarshan respectively. Her story *Un.kahi* was turned into a short film that won several awards, including Best Short Film at the Beijing International Film Festival. She has an eye for the right stories as a producer, as three of her productions – *Bittersweet, The Storyteller* and *The Rapist* – have won several awards, with the last-mentioned jointly winning the prestigious Kim Jiseok award at the 26th Busan International Film Festival. Two of her stories are currently underway to become feature films, written by some of the best names in the business.

The Silent Matter is her first collection of short stories.

For Aryan

Contents

1. SIX P.M. 1

2. A CUP OF TEA 27

3. A TALE OF TWO FRIENDS 57

4. ACROSS THE RIVER 79

5. ALL FOR LOVE 101

6. MOTHER 127

ACKNOWLEDGEMENTS 161

1

SIX P.M.

Deepti slipped the disposable plastic cap off her head as the clock struck seven. Her shift was over; it was time to go home.

Taking off her apron, she folded it neatly and put it into her bag. *Just like her mother*, thought Lalit, the bakery's middle-aged manager, as he watched Deepti clean up her station and get ready to leave.

Lalit had been a young man of nineteen and one of the first to be recruited when Sunrise Bakery had opened its doors thirty years ago, in 1980. Over the decades, he had worked his way up the ranks, going from menial kitchen duties to handling front-of-house, customer-facing responsibilities. His only friend at work, at that time, had been the twenty-six-year-old Renuka, a junior pastry chef. Despite her household and marital responsibilities – she came from a middle-class family, and had a three-year-old daughter – Renuka's work never flagged. Her eclairs and pineapple pastries became customer favourites.

Twenty-four years later, when Deepti, Renuka's daughter, also got a job at the bakery, everyone was ecstatic. "Now this truly feels like a family operation, Renuka didi," Lalit remembered saying. "We should have a team party for you and Deepti!"

He also remembered Renuka's tight smile at that time, and Deepti's lost expression. Little did he know that there was nothing to celebrate.

The year 2003 changed Deepti Malvade's life. Her father, Ashutosh, was diagnosed with early-onset Alzheimer's; her mother was inconsolable. This meant that the bulk of the managerial and caregiving duties – running from pillar to post, handling all of her father's medical requirements, from bills to medicines to doctor's appointments – fell on Deepti's shoulders. And it was all happening a mere four months into Deepti securing a position as a lecturer of economics at Pune University, a job she had worked tooth and nail to get.

So, for the next year or so, Deepti did the best she could. She carried out her teaching duties, took care of her father, and provided support to her mother, who wanted to resign from her position as Sunrise Bakery's senior pastry chef.

She did the best she could, till it was no longer feasible.

Even though her colleagues were understanding, Deepti was missing too many lectures. She was popular with her students, but the dean and the head of her department were beginning to show signs of dissatisfaction.

Her decision was cemented the day she rushed out of a lecture midway, for the third time in a week, to attend to a panicked call from her mother. Her father had wandered off, and was nowhere to be found.

During the stress-laden and interminably long autorickshaw ride back home, Deepti knew what she had to do.

Even though her father was home safe and sound when she reached – he had decided to take a stroll down the street, and forgot to tell his wife – she knew it was time to quit her job.

The university was on the other side of town; her mother's bakery, however, was just a fifteen-minute auto ride away from their house. They could even see it in the distance from their balcony.

"Aai," she told her mother that night, as they shared a quiet cup of tea together before bed, "can you call Lalit Sir tomorrow regarding that job?"

And so, in 2004, the twenty-seven-year-old Deepti gave up her teaching position, and joined Sunrise Bakery.

"She's following in Renuka's footsteps!" her mother's colleagues – and now hers – said. It was a matter of joy for them.

For her, it was the only way she could be close to home – close enough to rush back as and when summoned.

It was the only option she had left.

Six years later, these memories were still fresh in Deepti's mind. As she bid Lalit goodnight, she could tell, from the faraway look in his eyes, that he was thinking of her mother. She didn't blame him; she was thinking of Renuka too.

Her beautiful, caring mother, Renuka. Next month, Deepti thought, it would be two years since she died.

An overwhelming mess of anger, grief and longing swelled in Deepti's heart, as she sat quietly in the auto, heading homewards. She was furious at her mother for leaving her all alone in this world. She longed for her soothing touch. And she deeply missed the feeling of coming back home to her.

Now, she only had one person left in the entire world – her father. And while Deepti loved him deeply, and took great care of him, the bare truth was that he was no longer the person he once used to be. While his basic motor skills were still intact, he was lucid for only parts of the day. Sometimes, he did not even recognize his own daughter.

But Deepti had no choice – Aai had left Baba in her care.

So, over the past two years, she had built her own, quiet, little life – a life that revolved around the bakery, and her father. The only two things left in the world that she knew.

In the morning, after bathing and feeding her father, Deepti would let the maid in, give her instructions about the day's chores and her father's care, and then go off to work herself. For about an hour in the afternoon – the unofficial 'lunch hour' at Sunrise – she would come home, relieve the maid of her duties, and eat a quiet meal with her father. At four in the evening, when it was time for Deepti to return to work, a young student named Harish, from a nearby college, would arrive. Harish, one of the hundreds of cash-strapped young students trying to navigate college life in Pune, would take 100 rupees a day to keep the geriatric Ashutosh company from 4 to 7 p.m., Monday to Saturday. Although the fees were a bit steep, having someone to keep an eye on Ashutosh in the evening was the only way in which Deepti could continue working. Someone, after all, had to pay the bills – be it household expenses or medical costs.

Besides, her father seemed to enjoy Harish's company. They played Ludo and carrom together and went for a daily stroll, even though Ashutosh could rarely remember the young boy's name.

Every evening when Deepti returned, at about 7.20 p.m., Harish would take her leave. She would then set about cooking dinner. Father and daughter would sit and eat dinner in silence, each staring at the television. Attempts at conversation were mostly futile.

A couple of hours later, after helping Ashutosh brush his teeth and tucking him into bed, Deepti would retire to her own bedroom – one of two in their small flat.

There, alone for the first time in the entire day, Deepti would lie down with a book, trying valiantly to ignore the deep, gnawing loneliness eating away, bit by bit, at her heart.

Eventually, she would fall asleep, always aware that the next day – and the day after that, and the one after that – would be exactly the same.

And then, one day, it wasn't.

The day began and progressed as usual right up until the evening. It was not until she came home for the day, to the normal sight of Harish playing Ludo with her father, that the news was broken to her.

Harish was leaving.

"I graduate next month, Deepti didi," said Harish, sheepishly, as Deepti paced about the room, her face lined with worry. "I will be going back to Raipur, to join my father's business."

"Couldn't you have told me earlier?" Deepti asked him, her voice on edge. "It takes time to find a replacement, and I don't know when I'll get the time to look for someone new! Baba is already used to you ... and in his condition..."

"No, no, didi, don't worry!" Harish interjected. "We still have a month, right? You know that there are hundreds of students like me here in Pune, looking for a source of income." He looked at Deepti, his eyes serious. "You and Ashutosh Uncle have been so good to me. The least I can do is help you find someone who can take my place."

"All that is fine, but what if Baba does not take to him?" asked Deepti. Even she knew, deep down that Harish would have left sooner or later – he was, after all, just a student looking to make some pocket money. But they had fallen into such a comfortable rhythm of daily life, their routines moving like clockwork, that she had not thought far enough ahead to the day that he might actually quit.

"Do not worry about that, didi," Harish reassured her. "There are informal student networks all over the city for collegegoers on the lookout for jobs like this one. I will find someone trustworthy, and send them to you. If that does not work out, I'll find you someone else. There is also an agency

I know of that looks to connect young students with families searching for extra help. The bottom line is," said the young boy, "I won't leave without ensuring Uncle has someone to play Ludo with every evening."

Deepti looked at Harish, with his eager eyes and skinny frame, and her face finally cracked into a half-smile. "Alright," she said. "Help me find someone, then."

It was not long before they did.

Two weeks after their conversation, Harish called Deepti while she was at work. "Didi, I have a couple of pretty solid leads," he told her over the phone. "Shall we discuss this when you return tonight?"

"That would be great, Harish!" Deepti heaved a sigh of relief, but then composed herself. It would not do to seem too eager; Harish should not get the impression that she would hire the first person he sent her way. "We'll talk when I am back."

Later that day, Harish told Deepti about the leads he had managed to get. After he had spread the word, several possibilities had emerged – "the students really need money!" – but two stood out to him after he ran background checks. One was a young girl, an undergraduate studying geology at a city college nearby, who had approached him through the students' network. The other was a young man, doing his master's in biochemistry at the same college, but attached to the agency that Harish had spoken about. "If you meet him and decide he fits the bill, you'll have to go through the agency, didi," said Harish. "What would you like to do?"

Deepti chewed her lip for a couple of minutes, thinking about the best course of action. She glanced at the calendar.

Harish would be leaving in a little over two weeks' time.

She needed to hire someone suitable by then, so that Harish would have at least a couple of days to show them the ropes, and get her father used to their presence.

She would have to act fast. Do her due diligence, of course, but act fast.

"How soon can they meet me?" she asked.

Harish checked his phone. "The male candidate is free tomorrow, but you'll have to speak to the agency once," he said. "And the girl can come see you the day after that. Does that work?"

Deepti took a deep breath, then exhaled. "Yes," she said. "That works. Can you give me the agency's number please?"

The next day, at 7.30 p.m., Deepti was sitting across the dining table from a young man who looked nothing like a master's student. Yes, he was thin, tall, bespectacled and dressed like an impoverished student – kurta, pyjama and with a cloth bag full of books – but he was also impossibly handsome and definitely in his late twenties.

Looking at him was making Deepti's stomach do strange things. It was like her insides were doing somersaults.

But she decided to ignore these odd sensations. There were more important things to discuss.

"So, your name is Vineet Kumar?" she asked, looking through the papers that the agency had sent with the candidate.

"Yes, ma'am," he replied. The sound of his deep, slightly gravelly voice aggravated the weird sensations in Deepti's stomach. She cleared her throat. "And it says here that you are twenty-seven years old." She glanced at him. "May I ask why you are doing your master's so late?"

"Ma'am, I hail from Himachal Pradesh," replied Vineet. "After I finished my undergraduate degree, I had a few financial responsibilities towards the family to fulfil." His gaze dropped from Deepti's, and for a second, he looked downcast. "My father needed my help to get my two sisters married. So my studies had to be put on hold for a while."

He looked up, his face brightening again. "But now I'm back to studying," he said, his voice taking on a tinge of happiness. "I just started my master's, and am thoroughly enjoying it!"

His visible enthusiasm made it difficult for Deepti to mask a smile. Or to stop gazing at his face.

"As you know, my father has a fairly advanced degenerative condition," she said to Vineet, gesturing towards Ashutosh, who was seated in front of the television, gazing at the screen. "He needs patience and understanding, and, most importantly, he needs to feel comfortable. The job does not require much, but it will need vigilance, kindness and patience from your end. Do you think that is something you can manage?"

"Ma'am, Harish explained everything to me," said Vineet, looking in the direction of the old man. "I can assure you that I am the best person for the job." He stole a moment to glance at Deepti, and she felt her cheeks grow hot. "I lost my mother to Parkinson's," he said, quietly. "I know it is not the same thing, but if you give me a chance, you will see that I am good in these situations."

"I ... I'm sorry to hear that," said Deepti, her voice catching in her throat. Vineet's mention of his mother sent a searing pain of longing through her heart for her own.

Before memories of Renuka overwhelmed her, Deepti hastily moved on to other questions – where Vineet lived, what his class hours were, his day off in the week, and so on.

By the end of the interview, Deepti told Vineet that she would let him and the agency know if he was hired. But as she shut the door behind him, she already knew the answer.

She dialled Harish's number. When he answered, she told him that he need not send the other girl to her for an interview.

Two months had passed since Vineet had taken over from Harish – and, much to Deepti's delight, her father seemed to be the happiest he had been in the past two years. His face would light up every day when the doorbell rang at 4 p.m., and he would make the effort to get up from his chair himself to fetch the Ludo board and lay it out on the table.

Deepti was stunned at her father's change in demeanour. He had done none of these things when Harish was taking care of him.

Vineet, too, seemed genuinely happy to be in the old man's company. He would arrive every day with a smile on his face, a warm greeting for his senior friend, and a friendly challenge to beat him at Ludo or carrom. "Don't get too cocky, Vinesh, I'll beat you hollow today!" Ashutosh would quip, making Deepti smile. Her father may not get his companion's name right, but he certainly seemed a lot more invested in winning a game than he had been even a couple of months ago. Deepti happily noted that, every day, her father displayed the same energy levels at 7.15 p.m., when she came home, as he had when she left for work at 4 p.m.

"How do you do it?" she asked Vineet one day, gathering her things to leave while he set his own stuff down. "How have you managed to rejuvenate him so?"

Vineet smiled at her. "It's as you had said," he replied. "Patience, understanding, and he needs to feel comfortable. That's all I am doing." He turned around to look at her. "Besides," he said, softly, "I enjoy his company. And yours, for the few seconds in the day that our paths cross!"

Deepti felt the blood rush to her cheeks, and she managed to give him a tight smile before looking away. Her stomach was doing those furious somersaults again. What on earth was this effect Vineet had on her?

Her thoughts were interrupted by a good-natured bellow from her usually meek-voiced father. "Oi, Vinay!" he yelled. "What's taking you so long? Scared of losing, are you?"

Vineet and Deepti shared a glance before bursting into laughter. The last scene that Deepti saw, before closing the door behind her, was her father gleefully rolling the dice on the Ludo board, with his young companion, whose name he could never remember, sitting across from him.

As the weeks progressed, Vineet began to spend more and more time at the Malvade residence. Earlier, he would leave as soon as Deepti got home. One day, however, he asked if he could stay an hour longer. "Umm, yes, of course you can," said Deepti, her heart feeling inexplicably happy. "Don't you have to get home, though?"

"I live alone." Vineet smiled wistfully. "It gets lonely sometimes. I study most of the night anyway. So it's nice to be around Ashu Uncle ... and you." He looked up at Deepti, a sudden flicker of dismay in his eyes. "Unless you would like me to go! I'm so sorry, I do not mean to encroach upon your time with Uncle!"

"No no!" Deepti hastened to reassure him. "Please stay! It would make Baba happy." And her. It would make her happy too, although she could not say that out loud.

Unbeknownst to Vineet, Deepti's feelings for him had been growing unbidden, much to her dismay. She had never felt this way before, for anyone. The only other time was years ago, at the university. A fellow professor from a different department had expressed an interest in her, and even then, whatever she had felt for him was mild at best.

With Vineet, though, it was different. The mere sight of him made her day. And the sight of him leaving left her heart desolate, making the gnawing loneliness come rushing back.

She dared not let herself dream, but she often found herself longing to hold his hand. To lace her fingers through his, touch his cheek gently … run her fingers through his hair…

"Would you like some poha?"

Deepti nearly jumped as Vineet's voice broke through her reverie. "Wh … what?"

"Poha." Vineet was looking at her quizzically. "I made some at home. Please have some and tell me what you think?"

Stunned, Deepti took the bowl from Vineet's hands. It struck her that, a couple of weeks ago, she had mentioned to Vineet that she and her father had opposing likes and dislikes in food.

Like poha. He hated it, she loved it.

Deepti glanced down at the bowl. Vineet knew her father disliked poha.

Which means he had made it for her.

Her feelings all in a turmoil, it took Deepti all her courage to fight against her beating heart and look up to meet Vineet's gaze. When she did, a jolt of electricity shot through her veins.

She could have sworn his eyes mirrored what she was feeling. Could it really be?

It could not, could it? Deepti's mind was racing. Why would such a gorgeous young man be interested in her, a quiet, thirty-four-year-old loner with no life? It did not make sense to her – no matter how much she wanted it to.

Her thoughts were interrupted with Vineet taking the bowl back from her hands, scooping up a spoonful of poha, and offering it to her. "Taste, please?" Vineet said, his soft eyes holding her gaze. "I want to know what you think."

The intimacy of the moment stunned Deepti. She had never felt anything like it before.

There was nothing left to do but surrender to it. So she did.

The following weeks seemed to fly by in a haze of happiness in the midst of a burgeoning romance and growing intimacy. On some evenings, Deepti would come home to a delicious, hot dinner cooked by Vineet for her and her father; on other days, he would drop by her bakery at about 2.45 p.m., and wait for her break to begin, just so that he could take an auto ride with her back to her place.

Needless to say, everyone at Sunrise took a shine to him. This was the first time in years that they were seeing Deepti happy.

It was little things like this that touched Deepti's heart. In fact, on days when Vineet could not stay late, he would ensure Deepti, at the very least, came home to a freshly made cup of tea.

Those days were few and far between, though. It was now normal for Vineet to stay with the Malvades till well after dinner, chatting and laughing with father and daughter.

Before leaving, he would pull Deepti aside, away from her father's line of vision, and kiss her deeply. "Just so that you don't forget me," he would say, teasingly, before taking her leave.

The rest of Deepti's night would pass in delicious anticipation of Vineet's return the following day.

She could not remember the last time she had felt so happy. The thought astounded her. Is this what it felt like to be happy?

She decided to ask Vineet.

"Vineet … is this what happiness feels like?" she asked him the following day, her voice full of hesitation, as he stood in the kitchen making tea.

What she did not add was another, more important, question. One that she had not quite built up the courage to ask yet.

Would it last?

And there it was. The old, familiar, gnawing sadness. The loneliness. She still could not fathom why Vineet would want to be with someone like her.

"Yes."

Vineet's answer pierced through the haze of her inner voice.

"What?"

"I said, yes," Vineet replied, handing her a steaming mug of tea. "This is what happiness feels like." He looked at her tenderly as he tucked a strand of her hair behind her ear. "It's what I feel with you, every single day."

Deepti did not know how to respond, be it to his words that made her heart swell with joy, or to the frisson of excitement that his touch sent through her body. Overcome with a wave of shyness, she scuttled out of the tiny kitchen, with a wide smile on her face, the sound of Vineet's chuckles following her.

"I will get it for you! You have to give me some time, at least a couple of days!" Vineet sounded exasperated on the phone, as Deepti walked into the house at 7.30 p.m. He was sitting at the dining table, his hand on his head, a look of exhaustion on his face. When he spotted her, his eyes lit up, and he held out his hand. Wordlessly, she took it, and sat down next to him.

A few feet away from them, Deepti's father sat quietly, sipping a cup of tea and watching TV.

"Sir, I promise I'll get you the money. Just give me till the end of the week, please," Vineet was saying. 'It's just a matter of two days."

Who was he talking to? Deepti wondered. Seeing him so agitated was worrying her.

When he finally hung up, she gave him a few seconds to breathe before asking him what was happening. "Who was that?" she asked. "You sounded so distressed."

"My landlord," said Vineet, rubbing his temples with his fingertips. "My rent is due." Deepti could see the bags under his eyes.

"Are you short on funds this month?" she asked, hesitatingly. All she knew was that Vineet rented a one-bedroom barsati in a locality close to his college; beyond that, she had never really asked him about his living situation.

"You know how it is with these agencies," said Vineet. "They take the bulk of my earnings from this job, and whatever I have left goes in buying groceries and essentials." He suddenly looked up at Deepti, a look of guilt on his face. "But don't worry, I've got it figured out! A friend is lending me the money this month for the rent."

"But what after that?" asked Deepti. "You'll take a loan once ... and how will you pay it back? What about your subsequent months' rent?"

"I was thinking of giving tuitions," said Vineet. "If I can find about four to five students to take on, it would really help me supplement my income. In fact, I have an interview tomorrow with a prospective student's parents."

Deepti's heart felt full, looking at Vineet. She could not lie to herself: part of her had suspected that Vineet would ask her for the money to cover his rent. She banished the thought from her head, feeling guilty for even entertaining such a notion about her boyfriend.

Her boyfriend. That's what Vineet was.

It took Deepti a whole minute to let that thought sink in.

This gorgeous, loving man sitting across from her was her boyfriend.

At that moment, there seemed to be only one logical thing to do. The only thing that made sense to Deepti, and also filled her heart with joy.

"Vineet … do you want to come live with us?"

A whole minute of silence passed as Vineet looked at Deepti, stunned at her question. In that minute, Deepti could feel her heart disintegrate. Had she gone too far? Was it too soon?

"Deeps … are you sure?" Vineet asked, his eyes tinged with confusion. "Do you really want me to come live here with you and Ashu Uncle? Will it not be an extreme imposition?"

Deepti's heart leapt. He did not seem averse to the idea! "No, of course not!" she said, her words coming out in a rush of excitement. "Baba already loves you and is used to your presence. You spend most of your time here with us anyway. This way, you could save money, study, give tuitions, and we would have so much more time together." Her eyes sparkled, mirroring the evident joy in Vineet's eyes.

"I can set up a mattress for you in Baba's room … if you like." Deepti's eyes lowered, unable to meet Vineet's. He touched her chin, gently lifting her face. "I'll sleep wherever you want me to," he whispered. The butterflies in Deepti's stomach went into overdrive.

"So … does that mean you'll move in?"

"Yes, my love, I will. Thank you!"

That night, for the first time, Vineet helped Deepti put her father to bed. Then, he went on to spend his first night in Deepti's home, in a haze of desire and frenzied lovemaking.

As the lovers lay, spent, their limbs intertwined, Deepti gazed up at Vineet's perfect face, her breath catching in her throat. With a jolt, she realized she was deeply in love with this man … this wonderful man, who would, in a couple of years' time, finish his master's and leave Pune.

If he wanted to, Deepti decided, she would let him go.

It was enough that he had shown her what love is. What more could she have asked for, from her small, doomed life? She had already been given more than she deserved.

Almost as if he could read her mind, Vineet turned to face her, and wiped away the tears that she had not even realized were coursing down her face. "Deeps … you know I love you and that I will never leave you, right?" he asked, wrapping his arms around her.

"Even if you do, I'll always cherish this," she whispered. "You gave a lost girl a semblance of happiness, and a chance at love. I'll never forget it."

"Don't be silly," said Vineet. His voice was affectionate, but tinged with seriousness. "I am not playing around. I am here to stay." He lifted her chin to look into her eyes. "You and Ashu Uncle are my family. Okay? Now let's talk about when I can move in."

Up until now, Deepti had felt only love and joy. But now, for the first time, she felt hope.

"How about tomorrow?"

Vineet stared at her. "So soon?" he exclaimed. "Are you sure?"

"Absolutely," said Deepti. "It's Saturday. You don't have classes. You can go home, pack your things and bring them here."

Vineet's eyes flashed with joy. "That sounds … amazing!" he said. "I have very few things anyway; par for the course when you are a poor student." He turned to Deepti. "Tell you what; I have that interview with the student's parents early in the afternoon, so I could plan the day out like this: I go home, pack my things, deposit them at your office, then head for the interview. Once I am done, I collect my bag, and come back here. How does that sound?"

Deepti mulled the plan over in her head, before breaking into a smile. "That sounds good, my love!" She paused for a second, looking up at her lover's face. "I cannot tell you how excited I am."

"So am I," said Vineet, his voice laced with tenderness. "I can't wait to see what the future holds for us." He suddenly sat bolt upright, looking excited. "Deeps! Tomorrow night is technically our first night at home together, as … a couple."

He looked at her, his eyes shining with love. "Come home by 6 p.m. If you want, I'll speak to Lalit Sir. I want to make tomorrow night memorable for you … for us. No later than six, okay?"

Deepti giggled. She felt like a schoolgirl around Vineet. "You don't worry, I'll tell Lalit Sir I need to leave early," she said. "He'll be more than happy. Shall I bring your things back with me?"

"No need, I'll go get them myself. Wear something nice tomorrow," Vineet said, a smile curling at the edge of his mouth, sending a jolt of excitement and desire through Deepti. "Wear something nice, and wait for me."

Vineet had left by the time Deepti woke up, but he had placed a note and a rose next to her pillow. Unable to keep from grinning widely, Deepti set about her day, and left for work with a spring in her step. Since Vineet would not be able to make it for his 4 p.m. shift at her house, she had requested the maid to stay at home with her father till 6 p.m.

By afternoon, Vineet had dropped by the bakery, kept his luggage at the billing counter, charmed everyone all over again, and given Deepti a long hug. "I wish I could kiss you here," he whispered, "but I don't think society is ready for that just yet! See you at home at six sharp!"

As Deepti waved him goodbye, she felt contentment for the first time in her life.

Smiling, she walked back to her work station. Six p.m. could not come soon enough.

At 5.25 p.m., Lalit began to shoo Deepti away. "Go home, go home!" he said, affectionately. "No need to linger here!"

As Deepti got into the auto, she felt like the luckiest girl in the world. *I wish Aai was around to see me now*, she thought, a deep twinge of pain touching the edges of her joy.

When she reached home, she realized she still had a good twenty minutes left before Vineet arrived. After sending the maid away, she took a quick shower, dabbed on some of her favourite perfume, and took out a sari from the cupboard.

It was a beautiful Paithani. The first sari her mother had given her.

As she draped it, lovingly, she imagined what Vineet would say when he saw her in it.

Her heart filled with anticipation, she went and sat outside in the living room with her father. "Beta, how lovely you look!" Ashutosh exclaimed. "Just like your mother!"

Deepti smiled softly. Baba had noticed.

The clock struck six. Then six-thirty.

Deepti sat quietly with her father, a sliver of worry creeping into her heart. It was not like Vineet to be late. Was everything alright?

Even his phone was not reachable.

By 7 p.m., Deepti was frantic. Not knowing what to do, she turned to her father. "Baba, I'm worried about Vi—"

BOOM!

The sound of an explosion, the sonic might of which could not be described in words, blasted its way through Deepti and Ashutosh's soul.

Father and daughter sat in stillness – in deathly stillness – for what seemed like an eternity.

Their house seemed unharmed, but bits of debris that had blasted through the windows lay everywhere.

Deepti got to her feet unsteadily. Slowly, she made her way to the balcony.

And then she looked out at the horizon.

At the sight of a phantasmagoric cloud of shrapnel, fire, black smoke and ash. The place where Sunrise Bakery once stood.

See you at home at six sharp!

Inside, she could hear the TV come on. Her father had switched on the news.

Wear something nice, and wait for me.

Deepti stumbled back into the room. Her father was excitedly pointing to the TV screen, on which flashed Vineet's face.

Wanted terrorist, primary suspect, Sunrise Bakery bomb blast.

I go home, pack my things, deposit them at your office, then head for the interview. Once I am done, I collect my bag, and come back here. How does that sound?

"That's Vijay!" Ashutosh exclaimed, clapping his hands at Vineet's image on the news. "My friend Vijay! My friend is famous!"

I want to make tomorrow night memorable for you … for us.

In the distance, the wail of police sirens.

I can't wait to see what the future holds for us.

No later than six, okay?

2

A CUP OF TEA

Amit was intently reading what looked like an invitation card when his wife, Karuna, walked out onto the veranda with their morning tea. Without so much as a glance at her, he gestured to his wife to put his cup down on the small table next to him. Karuna obeyed.

"What's that you're looking at?" she asked, sitting down in the wicker chair next to him. The morning's newspaper was lying untouched on the table, she noticed, as she mixed half a teaspoon of sugar into Amit's cup.

Whatever he was looking at, it must be important, she thought. In all the years that they had been married, Amit never read anything in the morning before the newspapers – especially the one he owned.

"Amit," she pressed again, gently, "what's that you are holding?"

The middle-aged man tore his eyes away from the card in his hands, and looked at his wife, irritation writ large on his face. "What does it look like?" he almost barked. "It's an invite from my friend!" Before Karuna could respond, he dropped the card onto her lap and turned to his cup of tea.

Karuna picked up the invitation card and looked at it. Even though it was rather beautifully designed, her eyes caught, before anything else, the name of the sender on the envelope.

Urvashi.

Her brow furrowing just a little, Karuna scanned the rest of the text. Next to her, Amit noisily blew on his scalding hot tea in an attempt to cool it.

Join us for an evening of drinks, dinner, dance and song, to celebrate our 20th wedding anniversary! the card said. *We hope we will have the pleasure of your company on this joyous occasion.*

It was signed, *Pandit Upen Sharma and Urvashi Sharma.*

The date, time and venue were listed below.

Karuna felt puzzled as she read the words again, absent-mindedly reaching for her cup of tea with her other hand. *Has it really been that long*? she wondered. Had Urvashi really been married to Pandit-ji for twenty whole years?

Karuna was unceremoniously jerked out of her thoughts by a snarl from her husband. "Can you never do anything right?" he snapped, setting his cup down with such force that tea spilled out onto the saucer. "The tea is horrid! Why do you make it so strong? And would it kill you to add a little more sugar?"

Karuna took a deep breath, trying her best not to feel hurt. "Amit, you know I have to be careful about your intake of anything sweet," she said quietly. "The sugar levels in your blood reports..."

"Shut up! Always some excuse or the other." Amit glowered at her. "Why can't you just admit you can't do anything right?" Heaving himself out of his chair, the large-set man grabbed the newspapers from the table, and exited the veranda. "A man can't even hope for a decent cup of morning tea in this house!"

Karuna said nothing as she watched her husband disappear from sight. After two decades of marriage, she was used to this.

Trying to ignore the deeply buried hurt snaking its way up through her heart, she set down her own cup, still full, and went back to the kitchen to brew a fresh pot of tea for her husband.

As he settled down into the plush sofa in his palatial living room, Amit opened the papers, hoping they would help quell his irritation – both about his preferred morning beverage, and about his wife.

Ah, his wife. The unremarkable, plain, homely Karuna. Try as he might to focus on the business pages of his own paper, *The City Times*, Amit could not prevent his thoughts from racing back in time, twenty-two years ago, when his parents, the media tycoons Ajitesh and Amala Mukherjee, had broken the most unpalatable news to him: that he was engaged to be married. His bride-to-be? Karuna Ghosh – the younger, less pretty, introverted daughter of famed industrialist Barun Ghosh, whose deep pockets would certainly be useful in bolstering the declining fortunes of a print publication.

Amit recalled being livid at his parents when they showed him Karuna's picture. There was nothing he could do about the fact that his marriage was a strategic alliance – he had grown up knowing this would happen someday. But couldn't Baba and Ma have, at least, asked Barun Uncle for his elder daughter Bani's hand in marriage?

Amit had harboured a crush on Bani ever since they were in school, even though she was a couple of years older than him. She was everything Karuna was not – beautiful, extroverted, stylish.

The kind of woman a man would be proud to have on his arm.

But no – his fate with the dowdy Karuna was sealed. In fact, a year after their wedding, Bani stunned everyone by marrying an American, and left for the United States for good.

Amit could feel his irritation build just thinking about the past.

About the warning from his father, the night before his wedding. ("Treat your wife well. A lot of things, including your inheritance, depend on it.")

About the years that followed, where he climbed the ranks in his father's publication, and drowned himself in luxuries and the attention of other women.

About the day when he took over from his father as owner and chief editor of the media house – and the disdain he felt for his wife at the star-studded ceremony, sticking out like a sore thumb in her printed cotton sari amidst a sea of glamorous women in designer wear.

About the shame he felt when Karuna got a job as a schoolteacher. (The stupid woman held a PhD in physics, but had no ambition!)

About his decision to never have children with Karuna. How could he, when she looked like that? How could he be sure that his children would not turn out plain, short and overweight? (He satiated his desires elsewhere.)

About how he had absolutely nothing in common with his wife – be it in music, food or values. For instance, he loved ghazals and shayaris, but his wife had no understanding of music beyond Bollywood and popular Bengali music. In the early years of their marriage, when they were living in Mumbai, he had made the mistake of taking her to an expensive Italian restaurant. Her lack of appreciation for the food, that too in front of his friends, left him fuming. She was a downright embarrassment!

His tastes were expensive, hers were simple – a fact that deepened his disgust.

With all of these thoughts swirling around in his head, the sight of Karuna approaching him with a fresh pot of tea angered Amit even further. "*Abar birokto korte chole eshechho*?" (You've come back to irritate me?) he barked, causing her to almost drop the tray. "Can't you leave me alone for one damned second?"

"I … I just made you some fresh tea," she said, after regaining her composure. Taking a deep breath, she set it down on the table. "The sugar's on the side," she add quietly. "Be smart about it, please."

Before he could react, she handed him the invitation card. "Are we going for that?"

Forgetting the nasty jibe he had been preparing to throw at his wife, Amit immediately felt his heart jump when he saw the card again.

Urvashi. Oh, Urvashi!

"Yes, of course we are going," he said, not bothering to look at Karuna. "This is next week. If we have anything else scheduled for that evening, please cancel it."

"Alright," said Karuna, turning to leave. "I will."

"Oh, and remember," called out Amit, to Karuna's retreating figure, "please, for once, wear something classy! No cottons!"

Amit waited for the sound of Karuna's footsteps to recede. Then, he mixed two heaped spoonfuls of sugar into his tea and took a slow, long sip. "At least she got this round right," he muttered under his breath.

As he settled back, his large body sprawled across the sofa, the warmth of the *cha* seeping through his veins and calming his irritation, he allowed his mind to go straight to the reason for his buoyancy a few minutes ago.

Urvashi.

The captivating, gorgeous, ethereal Urvashi ... the woman of his dreams. Of every man's dreams.

Just the mere thought of her sent frissons of excitement through his body. A feeling, he was sure, was shared by every warm-blooded male in their social circle.

He felt just a tad bit jealous at the thought.

He could not wait to see her in a few days' time.

With glee, Amit picked up the phone and dialled Urvashi's number.

"I'm so glad you are coming, Amit-da!"

The sound of Urvashi's deep, throaty voice at the other end of the phone made funny sensations course through Amit's body. "I wouldn't miss it for the world," he said, eagerly. Then his voice dropped. "Karuna will also be coming," he said. "I hope that's alright."

"Of course, Amit-da!" trilled Urvashi. "Please bring her along. Although," she breathed, her voice conspiratorially dropping an octave or two, "you know I'm always happy to have you all to myself!"

Amit, his tongue in knots, could have passed out from the ecstasy.

"Well, I … I guess I'll see you soon then," he managed to stammer out. "Take care, Urvashi."

"Awww, can't wait," she drawled, on the other end.

Then she blew him a kiss on the phone, and hung up.

"Ramu, bring me another cup of tea!" Urvashi called out, as she dropped her mobile phone onto her lap and put her feet up. It was a beautiful sunny day in early December

– the perfect opportunity to sit out in the open, in her sprawling garden, sipping some ginger lemon tea and listening to the birds.

That's exactly what she was doing till Amit Mukherjee called, with his dog-like eagerness, to tell her that he would definitely be coming for her party.

Urvashi sniggered when she remembered the way his voice dropped when he mentioned his wife – what was her name? – would be coming along too. *Poor dear*, she thought. *His infatuation with me would be endearing if it weren't so pathetic*.

Not that she was complaining. Urvashi knew the effect she had on men.

And she had learnt, early on, that it was a remarkably useful tool to possess.

She smiled, leaned back into her lounge chair, and closed her eyes. Her thoughts began to wander so far that she didn't even notice Ramu setting her steaming cup of fresh tea down next to her.

Urvashi Patil had had a rough start in life.

Born into a lower middle-class family in Chembur, Mumbai, she had quickly developed ambitions well beyond their means. Both her parents worked secretarial jobs, but Urvashi discovered early on that she had a knack for acting and performing. From this discovery sprouted all her other desires – including the desire to become a renowned ghazal singer. She could not really tell if she had a singing voice, but she loved ghazals. She dreamed of getting her taalim from a pandit or an ustad, moving to an affluent part of Mumbai, performing around the world, and living in great luxury.

But haranguing her parents to pay for music lessons for her were of no avail. They simply could not afford it.

Worse, she soon learnt, the hard way, that being talented is not akin to being gifted – a truth she was forced to confront as she was passed over, again and again, for scholarship admissions to several music schools.

Not one to be fazed, however, Urvashi started learning on her own. Whatever her parents could not give her, she decided to give to herself.

And so, even as the years began to pass by, Urvashi began to relentlessly hone her talents. Mirza Ghalib, Mehdi Hassan, Begum Akhtar, Farida Khanum, Talat Mahmood, Jagjit Singh, Ghulam Ali – she studied the works and performances of all the greats, doing her best to emulate them.

Slowly but surely, she began to get bookings for singing gigs – first at neighbourhood functions and college fests, where the pay was negligible, and then, with time, at mid- to large-scale corporate events. She also started receiving invitations to poetry-reading sessions conducted among the upper classes of the city. Everybody seemed to want to hear Urvashi's shayaris, delivered in her signature, throaty style.

And so, as she spent more and more time performing, Urvashi discovered something else – men could not take their eyes off her.

They all wanted a piece of her – whether she was on stage, or off it.

What else could she do but make full use of this superpower?

Before long, the doyens of industry were eating out of her hands. Media moguls – including the son of the famous Ajitesh Mukherjee – were star-struck by her beauty and appeal, and wanted to do feature after feature on her. Record companies wanted to sign her on. The most high-end event organizers in India wanted her to do countrywide concert tours with them. Her fame in Mumbai's ghazal and poetry circles was rapidly increasing. She was on every guest list worth being on.

Soon, Urvashi even found herself making inroads into those hallowed bastions, almost impossible for outsiders to penetrate – the Hindustani classical and Carnatic circles.

It was at one of these events that Urvashi Patil met Pandit Upen Sharma – internationally renowned Carnatic vocalist, avowed bachelor, and eighteen years older than her.

Within the year, Urvashi had moved into his massive bungalow in Juhu. A few months later, they were married.

Everyone who was anyone, be it in the music industry or the corporate world, was stunned. No one, not even Pandit-ji's contemporaries and friends, could have anticipated this. They were all of the opinion that Urvashi had married him for his wealth and fame – but they were also well aware of the man's fondness for no-strings-attached female company.

How did he agree to the old ball and chain? This was the hot topic of conversation for weeks in the industry circles.

Eventually, everyone concluded that Urvashi had achieved the impossible. She must be special, the women said.

Oh, she is, said the men, conspiratorially. She most certainly is.

⁂

That was twenty years ago.

Urvashi smiled to herself as she finished the last sip of her tea. She was fifty-two, but did not look a day over forty. Standing up to stretch her long, shapely legs for a bit, she recalled the looks of envy and admiration in the eyes of the sea of people who had attended her wedding reception.

The women wanted to be her. But the men? The men just wanted her.

And she was okay with that. In fact, she welcomed it. Urvashi giggled when she remembered the moment she had brushed past Amit Mukherjee and whispered a soft sher into his ear. Even though his mousy little wife was standing right by his side, the man's face was almost comical in its ecstasy. She knew his weakness for shers and shayaris – she could tell that it took every ounce of self-control he could muster to not grab her that very moment.

For two decades, she had observed this effect she had on men. Even now, any room she walked into fell silent – just like the concert halls when she got onto the stage.

Just like the night of the wedding reception, when the gathering at her massive bungalow, including the media, had descended into a hushed silence as soon as she appeared with her husband. The only sound was the incessant click of cameras.

A grin tugged at the corners of Urvashi's rosy, lush lips. All those people would be there, once again, at her house the following Wednesday.

It was going to be one hell of a party.

Amit honked the horn of his car with the aggression of a bull. Simultaneously, he cursed Karuna through gritted teeth. Why couldn't the wretched sow hurry up?!

He'd been waiting in the car for ten minutes. They were supposed to have left for Urvashi's anniversary party half an hour ago.

It would take them at least an hour to reach Juhu. And every minute lost felt like a minute less he would have with Urvashi.

With a grunt of anger, he slammed the horn once again, and let it reverberate around the neighbourhood for a good ten seconds.

"*Ashchhi baba, ashchhi*! I'm coming!" Karuna called out, as she emerged from the main door and hobbled towards the car. Amit felt a slight twinge of guilt when he saw her; he'd forgotten that she had banged her foot into the leg of the table the previous night, and had been in pain ever since.

That fleeting feeling of sympathy for his wife disappeared, however, as soon as she sat next to him in the car and strapped on her seatbelt.

Even in a lovely red chiffon sari and muted gold blouse, with her hair done up nicely, Amit could not ignore how unattractive Karuna was to him.

He wished he could have divorced her years ago – but divorce, unfortunately, was not an option for him.

"Do you know how many times I honked?" he snarled at her, the startled look in her eyes making no difference to him. "Why are you late for everything all the time? Don't you know how long it takes to get to Juhu?"

"Amit, I … was just bandaging my foot," Karuna said. "We're only ten minutes later than we had decided. You don't have to speak to me so rudely all the time—"

"Just shut up!" Amit yelled, his anger beginning to bubble. Even he could not understand why he was getting so worked up.

Was it the Mumbai traffic? Or was it Urvashi? *It must be a bit of both*, he thought. *I've been looking forward to seeing her for days, but this woman is bent on creating delays for me*!

With a disproportionate amount of force, Amit revved up the car engine and shot out of their driveway.

Twenty minutes into the drive, the roads seemed to be surprisingly clear. Amit realized that they weren't encountering the usual amount of Mumbai traffic he had been fearing. With his mood gradually improving, he decided to switch on the radio. Conversation with his wife did not even cross his mind.

As soon as he set the knob to his favourite radio station, strains of *'Aaj jaane ki zid na karo'* emanated from it. But it was the voice that caught his attention.

Urvashi.

It was unmistakably Urvashi's voice.

Amit could feel his muscles tighten. Even after so many years, he marvelled at the effect she had on him.

The mere sound of her voice from a radio sent delicious shivers down his spine, causing him to grip the steering wheel harder. It reminded him of the sound of her voice – her sweet, tantalizing, breathy voice – whispering in his ear, the feel of her breath on his skin making the hair on the back of his neck stand on end.

So engrossed was he in Urvashi's vocals that it took a sharp prod from Karuna to bring him back to earth.

"What!" he mumbled irritably, feeling a tiny smidge of embarrassment. "Where did you disappear to?" Karuna asked, looking a bit concerned. "You were lost for a moment there."

"Oh it's nothing, I was just listening to the song," Amit said, fixing his eyes on the road. "Ufff, what a song! And what a voice! Urvashi's a legend."

Karuna looked at him out of the side of her eye, and contemplated whether to say anything. After a few seconds, she did.

"She's … not *that* great a singer, Amit," she said, cautiously. "I mean, she's not bad, but there are far better ghazal singers that we—"

"Oh please, you're just jealous!" laughed Amit, cruelly cutting her off. "What a woman she is!"

"Jealous?" asked Karuna, quietly. "Of what?"

"What else? Of her!" Amit exclaimed, still laughing. "All you women are jealous of Urvashi. You wish you could be like her!"

He did not even notice the hurt in his wife's eyes.

"I'm not jealous, Amit," she said, the calm in her voice not reflecting her hurt she felt inside.

"Really?" sniggered Amit, stealing a glance at his wife. "You're not jealous? Then why do you keep pointing out that she's not a good singer? Can you even be half of what she is?"

"I have no reason to be jealous," Karuna countered, looking out of the window, her face away from her husband. She looked out at the road instead, at the lights speeding by. "Everyone knows that it's all an act, a social drama that your ... *friend* lives in."

Amit ignored her.

"I hope we get to see Pandit-ji," Karuna said.

"And why won't we?" Amit asked, absent-mindedly, his focus still on the sound of Urvashi's voice.

Karuna turned to face him. "Have you forgotten the massive heart attack and stroke he suffered a few years ago?" she asked, slightly shocked. "I thought his wife was your friend!"

"She is," Amit snapped. "I must have forgotten. But yes, you're right, that was an unfortunate episode. He stopped singing after that."

"Yes, he had to," Karuna said. "It was all over the news. The attack really hampered his speech and motor functions.

He's barely made any public appearances since." She looked out of the window again. "Such a pity. He was – *is* – a national treasure."

"Yes, I suppose he is," Amit replied, not caring two hoots about his wife's words, or Pandit Upen Sharma, for that matter.

He was only going to the party for Urvashi.

The rest of the journey was spent in silence, save for Urvashi's voice blaring out of the radio.

By the time the Mukherjees pulled into the driveway of the palatial Sharma bungalow, they could tell that the party was already in full swing. As they walked towards the garden area, cameras flashed their blinding lights. Unused to being in front of the camera, the shy Karuna instinctively reached out for Amit's hand, for comfort.

To her horror, he shook her hand off. "What are you doing?!" he hissed. "There are people everywhere!" With that devastating show of cruelty, he swivelled on his feet and marched off in the direction of the gazebo, where everyone seemed to be heading.

It took Karuna no time to realize why.

Amit was, of course, making a beeline for Urvashi.

And, for a moment, even Karuna was stunned by her radiant beauty.

The ethereal Urvashi. Timeless in her shimmering silver sari and black lace choli. Showing off her sculpted body and ample bosom. Greeting guests with a dazzling smile. A touch here, a laugh there. The cameras were in love with her, just as much as the guests.

Everyone, as usual, was putty in her hands. Especially the men.

"Karuna!"

A loud, familiar voice broke through Karuna's reverie. She looked around to see who had called her name.

"Karuna, here! Look over here!"

Following the sound, Karuna finally spotted the person the voice belonged to. For the first time that evening, her face broke into a smile.

"Suchi!" Karuna walked as fast as she could towards that familiar face, grateful to have spotted a friend.

Suchi and Karuna had known each other since college, and Suchi's husband, the steel industrialist Suren Roy, was close to Amit.

It was Suchi who had first noticed Karuna's grief and misery owing to her marriage, and had befriended her. Suchi, too, knew what it was like to be shunned by her more successful, more famous husband.

Over the years, the two women had built a solid friendship, making the effort to meet as often as they could and share their lives with each other.

That is, until Suren bought a palatial home in Colaba, and moved there with his wife and children. That was nearly eight years ago. Since then, Suchi and Karuna barely got to meet.

"It's been so long, Karu," Suchi said tenderly. "Are you alright?" The kindness in Suchi's voice almost made Karuna cry, so unused was she to being spoken to nicely. But she bravely fought back her tears. She was doubly glad to have her friend's company this evening.

Not only did it give her time to catch up with Suchi, but it also made her feel less alone.

Her husband, after all, had abandoned her for Urvashi.

Where was Amit? Karuna looked around, trying to spot her husband. He was no longer at the gazebo. Neither was Urvashi.

Within seconds, she saw them – standing separately, Amit's face frozen in rapturous wonder as Urvashi laughed and spoke to him.

Almost as if she could tell she was being watched, Urvashi looked up, and locked eyes with Karuna. Instead of waving hello, she slowly lifted her finger and ran one manicured nail lightly down Amit's cheek, leaning in closer to whisper something in his ear, her sari slipping down her shoulder, as if on cue.

Karuna did not need to look at Amit to know what state he likely was in at that moment.

Her heart filled with misery, Karuna turned back to Suchi.

"Hey, what are you ladies talking about?" Suren and Amit, drinks in hand, sauntered up to the table where their wives were sitting, and plonked themselves down. It was evident that they were already drunk. "C'mon, tell us!"

"Oh, nothing really." Suchi smiled tightly. "Just talking about school and the kids—"

"Hey, look there!" Suren cut off his wife, pointing in the direction behind her. The other three turned to look.

Urvashi, amidst a blinding flash of camera lights, was carefully guiding her husband, in his wheelchair, into the garden. She was followed by two young men in uniform, possibly his attendants.

One by one, everyone at the party turned to look at Urvashi and Pandit-ji. The chatter all around the garden died down.

As Karuna watched, Urvashi brought the wheelchair to a halt, ensuring that her husband faced the gathering. Magically, from somewhere, a microphone appeared in her hand.

Urvashi, on stage, mic in hand. Karuna could already tell that she was in her element. There was pin-drop silence all around. Everyone's gaze was transfixed on the angel in black and silver standing in front of them.

With graceful, measured movements, Urvashi tapped the mic. Satisfied that it was on, she brought it to her shimmering red lips.

"Twenty years ago, almost all of you were here, on this very lawn, to share in our joy and bless your beloved Pandit-ji and me for the journey we were about to embark upon," she said, looking slowly around the crowd, her eyes lingering now and then one someone or the other. "Today, the party is larger, filled with friends that Upen and I have made over the last two decades. But apart from the size of the gathering..." Urvashi paused, then slowly turned to look at her husband, placing her hand tenderly on his shoulder. "...the only other thing that has grown over the years is the depth of our love."

Five seconds of silence, as she watched her words sink into the crowd.

Then, thunderous applause.

Even Karuna was transfixed.

As the applause died down, Urvashi bent down towards her husband, her pallu, once again, slipping from her shoulders. The slight murmur that rose among the audience – the men – was quelled within seconds by icy glares from their wives.

"Upen, would you like to say a few words to your friends here?" Urvashi asked lovingly, fixing her pallu and proffering the mic to her husband.

Pandit-ji, with his head drooping, made no sound. His eyes fluttered open for a few seconds, and it seemed as though he wanted to say something. But he gave up the attempt quickly, and closed his eyes again.

Whispers of concern and distress began to make the rounds among the crowd – although they knew that he was mostly immobile, few among them had seen Pandit Upen Sharma in this state before.

Straightening up, Urvashi quickly took the mic back. "As you all can see, Upen has not been keeping well," she said, her voice a perfect, almost practised, mix of cheer and gravity. "But there's no cause for worry. I am always, always there by his side – together forever."

Amid cries of "how sweet!" and "awwww", Urvashi leaned down to plant a kiss on her husband's head.

Several feet away, much to the disgust of Karuna and Suchi, the men were performing a balancing act of salivating over Urvashi's cleavage and lamenting over the fact that she was married to a man like her husband. "I can't believe she's married to that … that *cripple*!" Amit slurred. "What a bloody *WASTE*!"

"Amit, calm down!" Karuna implored, deeply embarrassed. "Everyone can hear you!" Then, unable to help herself, she asked, "What do you mean, *waste*?"

Amit looked at her, unconcerned that he was talking to his wife. "You know what I mean," he sneered, taking another swig of his whiskey, as Suren chuckled alongside him. "All of that beauty, those lips, that body … wasted on a man like him."

Karuna immediately regretted asking that question. Sensing her pain, Suchi reached out from under the table and squeezed her hand in sympathy. Both women looked on as Urvashi cut a cake and blew out candles with her husband, who needed help from his attendants to even hold the knife.

As the evening wore on, Karuna watched the tall, statuesque Urvashi flit from table to table, talking to her guests, charming them with her wit and smile. She really knows how to make people feel important, Karuna thought, her eyes following every contour of Urvashi's swaying body as she walked around the lawn.

Suddenly, a commotion drew Karuna's attention towards the table where Upen was seated. From what she could tell, he had dropped food all over his lap.

In the blink of an eye, Urvashi, in her shimmering glory, was by his side. Pulling up a chair next to him, she shooed away his attendants, and began cleaning the gravy off his clothes.

Then, much to everyone's awe, she proceeded to feed her husband with her own hands, gently and lovingly coaxing small morsels into his mouth, paying no heed to the food stains gathering on her own designer sari, which everyone knew must have cost several lakhs.

As she wiped his mouth with a napkin, there was not a dry eye in the crowd. Including Karuna's.

"Maybe ... maybe I was a bit quick to judge her," Karuna said in a low voice to Suchi. Amit, unfortunately, heard her. "Yeah, you were," he snorted with laughter. "'I told you that you were jealous! Face it, Urvashi's perfect." He turned his eyes back to the object of his affection, and sighed. "What man wouldn't crave a wife like that?"

At that moment, Karuna hated herself for agreeing with her husband.

Soon, Urvashi stood up, and turned to her guests. "It's time for Upen to get some rest," she said, smiling at everyone. "He may not be able to say it himself, but he is so very grateful to each of you for coming today. But, please, do not go anywhere!" She gestured to the DJ to start playing the music again. "The party isn't over, I'll be back in no time!"

Something, in that moment, came over Karuna – and, much to Amit's horror, she stood up, and addressed Urvashi directly. "But, Urvashi," she said, as the crowd hushed again, "won't the noise from the party disturb Pandit-ji? How will he sleep?"

"Oh, sweet Kamini, do not worry about that at all!" Urvashi tittered, unaware and uncaring that she got Karuna's name wrong. "He'll sleep tonight in the furthest wing of the bungalow, so that nothing can disrupt his rest." She fixed Karuna with a steely stare. "Why don't you have a drink and just enjoy the party, dear?"

With that, the silver angel departed, pushing her husband's wheelchair towards the house.

Karuna bore her husband's tirade stoically for the next ten minutes. She knew he'd stop as soon as Urvashi returned.

It was 7 p.m. the following evening when Karuna, finally done with correcting test copies, sat down to take a breather. Amit was at work and had said he would be late. Was that a lie? Was he secretly going to meet Urvashi?

Karuna was so tired, she did not even care.

She had just grabbed the remote and switched on the television when her phone rang.

Suchi was calling.

Her face breaking into a smile, Karuna pressed the answer button. "Suchi!" she said, happiness evident in her voice. "I'm so glad you called. *Bolo, ki khobor?*"

"Karu." Suchi's voice on the other end sounded serious. "Have you heard?"

"Heard what?" Karuna was genuinely confused. "What's happened? Is everything alright?"

Over the next two minutes, as she listened to her friend talk, all the colour drained from Karuna's face.

That night, she went to bed without eating dinner. Even when she heard Amit return at 3 a.m., she did not get up.

It was only in the wee hours of the morning that Karuna had managed to fall asleep. Thus, by the time she awoke it was already 8 a.m. In a panic, she rushed to prepare Amit's tea.

When she went out onto the veranda, Amit was staring out at their garden. The newspapers lay untouched in front of him.

As she set the tray down, Amit's phone rang. Before he answered, Karuna saw that it was Suren calling.

"Hi, Suren," said Amit, his voice sombre. "Yes, yes, I heard. I found out last night, in the office. It's truly terrible. I can't believe a woman like her could do such a thing." He glanced at Karuna pouring his tea, a peculiar look in his eyes. "Listen, Suren, can I call you back later? My wife's here, I need to speak to her. Yes, sure, let's talk tomorrow."

As Amit disconnected the call, Karuna wondered whether what he wanted to talk to her about was the same thing that Suchi had told her the night before.

"Did … did you hear?" Amit asked, hesitatingly. Karuna nodded. "Suchi told me. How did *you* find out?"

"One of our reporters," Amit replied, rubbing his eyes. "He was in the media corner that night, covering the party."

Karuna took a deep breath. "Amit," she asked quietly, "is all of it true? All of it?"

"I'm afraid so."

"How did your reporter find out?"

Amit looked deeply uncomfortable for a minute. And then, he told his wife the whole story.

About how the *City Times* reporter and cameraman stealthily followed Urvashi while she wheeled her husband back into the bungalow. About how, away from all eyes, she and the two attendants then emerged at the back of the house, loading the paralysed man onto a stretcher and into an ambulance.

About how, while Urvashi returned to the party, the ambulance took the old man far away, to an old-age home on the shady outskirts of the city, where he had been languishing for the past seven years.

About how a nightlong investigation revealed two things: one, that Urvashi had, two years ago, managed to get the entire Juhu property transferred to her name, and had been living there by herself while her husband rotted away in an anonymous corner of the city. And two, she had sold the bungalow, just two months ago, for an eye-watering sum of money.

And, finally, about how, in the early hours of this morning, Urvashi was spotted at the airport with a tall, Middle Eastern man – conjectured to be her lover – leaving for Dubai.

For what seemed like an eternity, Karuna sat quietly, her mind in shreds as she tried to make sense of everything Suchi and Amit had said.

Finally, she spoke. "So … the party last night … was it all…"

"Yes," said Amit, looking downcast and very embarrassed. "It was clearly just a front, to fool people into thinking she's a caring wife and that they have a happy marriage. And the worst thing is" – he cleared his throat uncomfortably – "we fell for it."

"We did, didn't we?" murmured Karuna. "We all did."

She got up, ready to throw herself into work. Anything to distract herself from the horrors she had just learnt about.

"Karuna?" Amit's voice stopped her just as she was about to go inside.

"*Bolo*," she said. "Anything you need?"

"No, nothing," he said, his cup of tea in his hands. "I just wanted to say … Thank you for the tea. It's very nice."

As Karuna looked at her husband, something, after all these years, shifted between them.

A few hundred kilometres away, in a dingy room at the corner of the old-age home, a young orderly shoves a cup of tea into Pandit-ji's trembling, unstable hands. "Don't you dare spill a drop today, old man," he barks. "There's no one to clean up after you!"

Pandit-ji cannot help it. His tea spills everywhere.

Unlike Urvashi's wine, which she sips at leisure, several thousand miles, mountains, and seas away, in the heart of Dubai, her beautiful legs outstretched on the veranda, as she looks out at the city.

3

A TALE OF TWO FRIENDS

The bell atop the door of the salon tinkled at exactly 11 a.m. on that Tuesday morning. The sound of it made Gargi's heart jump with joy. She didn't even need to look up from her chore to know who it was. But, wait … could it really be?

"I'm here!"

Gargi, who was styling a client's hair, switched off the hair dryer and turned around. There stood Leena, and the sight of her smile gladdened Gargi's heart. "Leena-di!" Gargi squealed. "You're back!" If professional decorum had allowed, she would have rushed to Leena and hugged her. "*Eto din kothaye chhile*? It's been months!"

"I had some crucial work to finish," said Leena, quickly setting down her bag. "Will you be long?"

"I'm almost done." Gargi smiled. "Take a seat, give me five minutes."

"Take your time!" said Leena, settling into the swivel chair next to where Gargi stood. "I have all morning and all afternoon."

Gargi chuckled, and switched the dryer on again. She felt a sharp burst of happiness – it was so good to have Leena back after six whole months!

Leena was Gargi's favourite client. Well, she was everybody's favourite at the salon – she was beautiful and cheerful, she came in regularly, tipped generously, and, most important, spoke to everyone warmly. That, frankly, was something that Gargi and all her colleagues valued even more than the tipping – especially after having to deal with rude, and sometimes downright ill-behaved, clients all the time.

But even though everyone at the salon wanted to wait on Leena, it was Gargi that she seemed to prefer. In fact, Gargi would even go so far as to call it a friendship. Whenever Leena called to book an appointment, be it for a facial or a massage, she would always ask for Gargi. And if Gargi was not free, she would delay or even postpone the appointment.

To a certain extent, all of this made Gargi the envy of her colleagues. But she did not care; the manager was pleased because, according to him, Gargi was bringing in frequent business from a regular client ("She came three times this week, and she always asks for you! Good job, Gargi!"), and his approval meant that she could, perhaps, hope for a passably decent appraisal in a few months' time.

But more than that, even more than the hopes of a pay rise, it was the peculiar bond that she seemed to have formed with Leena that made Gargi happy. For Leena, even though she was a client in a professional setting, treated Gargi like a close friend.

She told her everything.

So Gargi knew all that there was to know about Leena – about her childhood, spent in the beautiful mountain town of Kurseong with two nannies because her parents were almost always in the city on work; about her schooldays, where she had only two friends owing to her quiet nature; about her final move to Kolkata at the age of eighteen to begin college, where she blossomed, excelled, and met the love of her life; and, of course, about Ritesh.

Ritesh was the aforementioned love of Leena's life. They had been together since her second year in college, and had married soon after they both completed their master's degrees. Both hailing from wealthy families, Leena and Ritesh led a very comfortable life together – they had been married for twelve years, had a thriving social life, and lived close by, in one of the city's poshest gated communities. Up until a year ago, they would go on holidays abroad twice every year, till Ritesh had a mild heart-related scare. "Thankfully it was mild," Leena had told Gargi, "but the doctor advised both of us to take it easy on the constant travel for about a year or so."

But what was most evident was how much Ritesh doted on Leena. Gargi smiled as she set up the masseuse's table, recalling the time, about two years ago, when Ritesh had come to pick Leena up from the salon. They were supposed to go to the wedding reception of a big industrialist's son, but Leena's hair and makeup for the event were taking forever.

Gargi remembered how Ritesh, fully dressed and looking incredibly handsome, came and sat at the salon, waiting patiently for his wife. Men have certainly opened up to the idea of personal care and grooming for themselves over the past decade or so – but even now, most men, Gargi thought, wouldn't be caught dead *waiting* at a salon for their girlfriends, mothers, wives, sisters or daughters to finish getting their hair or nails done.

Gargi, however, remembered Ritesh not only telling Leena to take her time, but also looking like he had fallen in love with her all over again when she saw her emerge, resplendent and ready to go. Gargi wasn't the only woman in the salon who felt a twinge of jealousy that day – all of them wanted to be treated like that by their partners! Gargi would never forget the look of utter joy on Leena's face that evening, as she left with Ritesh for the reception.

Today, too, Leena seemed to be excited about something – and, as Gargi observed her getting ready for her massage, she could tell it was about Ritesh. "How have you been, didi?" she asked, as Leena lay down on the massage table.

"The same as I was when you last saw me!" Leena laughed.

"Didi, that was more than six months ago," Gargi reminded her gently. "We have all really missed you here. Where were you…"

"In fact, I would have come yesterday, but your dada had other plans." Even while massaging her shoulders, Gargi could tell that Leena was smiling while talking about Ritesh.

"Ooo! Did Sir plan something special for you?" asked Gargi. It was moments like this that she treasured the most – it was a special privilege to have someone open up to you enough to share their innermost thoughts and feelings about their partner. "Tell me everything!"

"How many times have I told you, don't call him 'sir'," chided Leena good-naturedly.

"Okay, okay, I won't," Gargi laughed. "Now tell me!"

"*Arre, ki je bolbo*! What can I say? Your Ritesh-da is too much." Suddenly, she gestured to Gargi to stop, and sat up abruptly. For a second, Gargi was alarmed – did she accidentally hurt her client? – but noticed Leena's expression and stopped. She was smiling shyly.

"I haven't told anyone this, but Ritesh and I have been talking about having a baby," Leena said, blushing furiously. "We've decided that it's time to grow the family. He is doing much better health-wise, and the break from travelling has helped us think about the future in more concrete terms."

She finally looked up at Gargi, who was listening to Leena with wonder.

"Didi!" Gargi almost yelped with joy. "That is such wonderful news! Are you pregnant?"

"No no, not yet!" Leena let out a full-throated laugh. "We only just made the decision last night..." Her words trailed off, but her face beamed.

"So ... did sir do anything special for you to celebrate?" asked Gargi playfully, gently helping Leena lie down again.

"*Ufff, ki je bolish tui*! Stop teasing!" giggled Leena. "But your dada – not sir! – really is too much! I wanted to cook him a special meal yesterday, to celebrate our decision..."

"*Arre wah*, didi!" Gargi interjected. "What did you make for him?"

"*Bolchhi, shob bolchhi, ektu* wait *kor*," Leena laughed. "I'll tell you everything! Your dada loves Chinese food, so I thought I'd make some Kung Pao chicken and egg fried rice for him."

The mere mention of this made Gargi's stomach rumble with hunger – she loved Chinese food too.

"It must have been delicious na, didi?" she asked. "Just thinking about it is making my mouth water!"

Leena giggled. 'I don't know. I don't eat Chinese food," she said. "But Ritesh loved it! He is not allowed to eat red meat anymore, so I've been doing my best to make chicken, fish and egg preparations interesting for him."

"You don't like Chinese food?" asked Gargi, continuously massaging Leena's head. "Then what did you eat?"

Leena paused. Gargi considered repeating her question, but decided not to. By now, the two of them had developed a rhythm, an understanding ... she instinctively knew when Leena would speak, and when she would quieten down. Their banter was seamless, but even their silences were comfortable. Like old friends.

A minute or two later, Leena spoke up. "Making Ritesh happy was, honestly, my only concern yesterday," she said, softly. "That's why I wanted to cook him Chinese food. But you know your dada. He always has a surprise up his sleeve for me."

"Oh, this is exciting!" Gargi squealed. "What was the surprise?"

Leena smiled. "I should have known that he would think about making the evening special for me as well." Her eyes sparkled like those of a girl newly in love. "It so turns out that while I was busy in the kitchen putting together his Chinese favourites, Ritesh was secretly ordering pasta for me from my favourite Italian restaurant!" She closed her eyes, a smile touching her lips. "He wanted both of us to eat what we like, together."

Gargi felt a pang in her heart. Ritesh Sir loved Leena-di so much! It was almost magical witnessing their love through Leena's eyes. She treasured these moments of sharing, and had sorely missed them for the months that Leena was gone. These moments made her feel like she was a part of Leena's life – an important part.

Gargi knew enough about the world to be aware that, outside the walls of the salon, someone of Leena's social background would never be able to maintain and nurture a proper friendship with someone like her. They belonged to vastly different worlds – Leena lived in prosperity with her husband in a plush home, the universe at their fingertips, while she, Gargi, lived from paycheque to paycheque, returning every night to a one-bedroom rented apartment that she shared with her mother.

And yet, within the walls of the salon – indeed, within the walls of the spa room – was a world where she and Leena were true, genuine friends. Friends who told each other everything, friends who shared their hopes, dreams, sadnesses and innermost thoughts. And she knew Leena felt the same way – if anything, it was Leena who made Gargi feel like she mattered.

"What are you thinking?" Leena's words broke through Gargi's reverie.

"Oh, nothing really – just wishing my boyfriend were half as romantic as Ritesh sir!" Gargi said, jokingly, as she resumed the massage. "Perhaps I should send him to sir for training! What do you think?"

Leena looked up from her supine position at Gargi, her eyes flashing with some unreadable emotion. "Don't say that, Gargi," she said, in a low voice. "Shabbir loves you in his own way. I see the way he comes to pick you up after work from here … much to the chagrin of Surya, might I add!"

Gargi rolled her eyes at the mention of Surya – the salon's magazine delivery boy who had a huge crush on her, and was known to look for any excuse to drop by the salon for a glimpse of her.

"*Uffff* didi, why are you mentioning him?" complained Gargi, while Leena chortled. "You know how the sight of him irritates me!"

"I know, I know." Leena laughed. "I was just teasing you." Her voice trailed off, and she closed her eyes. "All I am saying is that Shabbir does love you."

"Hmm, maybe you're right, didi," responded Gargi, considering Leena's words. "He *does* show me he cares, in his own way. Besides, I guess, not everyone can be the same."

"That's right," said Leena, her eyes still closed, but with laughter in her voice. "No one can be like Ritesh!"

The sound of the two women's laughter in the spa room could be heard everywhere in the salon.

At the end of the day, when Shabbir came to pick Gargi up, Riya, the receptionist, noted the marked difference in Gargi's reaction to the sight of him.

"*Kya baat hai*, Gargi?" she said, teasingly. "It's been a while since you've looked so excited to see Shabbir!" She glanced out the door, where the young man was waiting on his motorcycle. Then she looked back at Gargi, and smiled knowingly. "Leena-di said something to you, didn't she?"

Gargi swatted Riya away affectionately. "Keep quiet!" She laughed, as she walked out the door. "We'll talk tomorrow."

⁂

It was three days later that Leena came to the salon again. As the tinkling of the bell announced her arrival, Gargi felt a sense of calm wash over her. Oh, how she looked forward to Leena's visits!

"Come and sit, didi." Gargi didn't miss a beat. "Do you want a cup of tea before we get started..."

"Gargi! Listen to me!" Leena cut her off. "Today is my wedding anniversary!"

Gargi's face broke into a huge smile. Her heart warmed up to see Leena's child-like excitement at the prospect of her anniversary ... even after thirteen years of marriage!

"That's so exciting, didi!" Gargi clapped her hands in glee. "This calls for something special. Something luxurious. Perhaps a new haircut with some highlights? A nice manicure? A gold facial?"

"All of that and more." Leena smiled. "I want you to give me a makeover. I need to look my best tonight for Ritesh! He's in Mumbai for work, but is returning in the evening. When he comes home, I want him to feel the way he felt when he saw me for the first time."

Her words almost made Gargi tear up. It was rare, so rare, to witness a love like this … two people, married for years and years, facing the wear and tear of life together, yet just as much in love now as they were when they met over a decade ago.

It was every person's dream, a love like theirs.

"Say no more, didi." Gargi smiled at Leena. "You are in good hands."

"I know I am. I only trust myself with the best." Leena winked at Gargi. "Now, tell me what we are starting with."

As Gargi readied all her equipment, she observed Leena, merrily chatting with Riya and some of the other girls, radiant with joy. She wondered what Ritesh had in mind for their anniversary. Was he also getting himself groomed for her? Would he cook for her? Would he take her out, get her flowers?

Almost as if she had read her mind, Leena started telling Gargi about the flowers that had arrived at her doorstep in the morning. "I opened the door after I heard the bell, and there stood a delivery man carrying this huge bouquet of roses!" she exclaimed, while Gargi trimmed her hair. "It was stunning, and the message that Ritesh wrote on the accompanying card…" Leena paused, a lump clearly forming in her throat. "I don't think I've ever received a more romantic message from him."

Gargi was enthralled, listening to Leena speak. "He's such a gentleman, didi!" she said. "Sending you your favourite flowers first thing on your anniversary morning, even though he is away. Must be such a wonderful feeling."

"Oh, roses aren't my favourite." Leena laughed. "Lilies are."

"Then why didn't sir get you lilies?" asked Gargi, puzzled.

Leena looked at Gargi through the mirror's reflection. "Sometimes, receiving something that your partner loves is as fulfilling as getting something that you love," she said, softly. "He loves roses, and believes that they signify the entirety of love better than any other kind of flower." She paused, her eyes suddenly faraway. "Love is a matter of give and take," she said, after a few seconds. "And that's as it should be."

She suddenly brightened up again. "*Janish*, Gargi, the flowers are sitting on my dining table as we speak, and the whole house is filled with the beautiful smell of roses." She laughed. "I can't wait to go back home." She closed her eyes. "I can't wait for Ritesh to come home."

"Be patient, didi, there's still a lot left to do," Gargi joked, preparing the hair colour mix for Leena's highlights. As she did, she stole a glance at Leena's beautiful face, lost in thought, and felt a wave of affection for her friend. "Didi," she said, gently putting her hands on Leena's shoulders, "henceforth, please don't stay away for so long. Your presence brightens up this place and our lives. We don't like it when you're not here."

Leena chuckled. "I promise, Gargi," she said. "I won't disappear again. I missed you too." She looked at Gargi. "Talking to you gives me peace."

Four hours later, Leena looked like a vision – even more beautiful than before, if that were possible. Her skin glowing, her eyebrows perfectly shaped, her hair shining with bounce and new burgundy highlights, her nails immaculately done … no one at the salon, from employees to clients, could take their eyes off her as she emerged from the spa section and headed towards the billing counter.

"Ma'am, *aap bohot sundar lag rahe hai*," said Riya, shyly, as she rang up Leena's bill. "Absolutely gorgeous."

Leena's face flushed with pleasure, and Gargi could have sworn that her eyes teared up a little. "Thank you, Riya," she said, warmly. "I hope your Ritesh bhaiya says the same thing!"

"He will," Gargi interjected. "How can he not? His wife looks like a supermodel!"

"All thanks to you," said Leena, suddenly emotional. She clutched Gargi's hands in hers. "I really appreciate everything that you have done for me, Gargi. Can't wait to see you again tomorrow." Her eyes flashed naughtily, and her voice dropped to a whisper. "When I'm back, I'll tell you all about tonight!"

Gargi giggled like a schoolgirl, thrilled to be part of Leena's inner world. "I'll be right here waiting, didi." She grinned. "Oh, and before you go…" She quickly reached into her pocket, brought out a small glass bottle, and pressed it into Leena's palm.

"What is this?" asked Leena, looking at the vial.

"It's a gift from me." Gargi smiled warmly. "It's a lovely, oil-based fragrance that I found. I think it would be perfect for you to use on your anniversary night." She paused, before saying, "I think Ritesh sir would *really* appreciate it."

Leena didn't say anything for a few seconds. Gargi looked away, suddenly embarrassed, and a little bit scared. Had she crossed a line? Leena was, after all, a client – no matter how much Gargi viewed her as a friend. As Leena kept looking at the bottle, Gargi spotted Surya enter the salon, and felt a jab of irritation alongside her fear. Just my luck, she thought. Leena's offended, and now I'll have to bear Surya's annoying presence as well!

"Gargi, I'm so lucky to have a friend like you." Leena's words pierced through Gargi's anxious thoughts. She looked at her favourite client – her friend – and saw her eyes shining with gratitude. Instantly, she felt a load lift off her chest. Leena liked the gift!

"I love the fragrance!" Leena exclaimed, taking a whiff of the perfume. "I'm sure Ritesh will *really* appreciate it too." She winked at Gargi, who blushed and giggled. Even the feeling of that good-for-nothing Surya's eyes on her could not shake her feeling of euphoria at this moment.

In the midst of her whirl of feelings, she felt Leena slip something into her hand as well. Puzzled, Gargi glanced at what she held in her fingers, and then looked up in shock.

Three thousand rupees! Was this a tip?

"I remember you telling me you love Chinese food, right?" Leena smiled. Gargi, with words stuck in her throat, could only nod. "Well then, tonight, Shabbir and you are going out for a nice Chinese dinner."

Before Gargi could form the words to thank her, Leena had turned around to leave. At the door, she looked back at Gargi one last time. "Pick a nice place," she said. "I want to hear all about it when I come back."

Her eyes still shining with gratitude, Gargi nodded vigorously. "You have fun with Ritesh sir tonight, didi!" she said.

"Ufff Gargi, it's dada, not sir!" Leena laughed. "And yes. I will."

With a last wink and a smile, Leena left.

"I can't believe she gave you a 3,000-rupee tip!" Riya said to Gargi, slightly envious. "Shabbir and you are going to stuff your faces with Chinese food tonight, aren't you?"

The two girls were still gossiping and gushing over Leena and Ritesh when Surya cautiously sidled up to them. "*Ei* Riya, go through the magazines stack *na*," he said. "Pick what you need. Then I can take the rest back with me."

The mere sound of his voice annoyed Gargi. "Can't you see we are talking?" she snapped at him. "Leave us alone."

Surya was so in love with Gargi that even the harshest words from her sounded like music to his ears. Her demand that he leave them alone flew over his head.

"Yes, I did overhear you both talking," he said. "About a client and her husband. Who were you talking about?"

Gargi was about to bark at him to mind his own business, but Riya pipped her to the post. "Leena Ma'am and her husband Ritesh," she said, eagerly. "Everyone here loves her. She just left ten minutes ago. She came and prepped all day for her anniversary celebration, which is tonight!" She looked at Surya. "You must have seen her," she said. "You were standing right next to the door when she left."

"Riya, that's enough," Gargi said, already irritated with the receptionist for volunteering so much information. She then turned to Surya to tell him to make himself scarce – but her words died in her throat when she looked at his face.

Surya was looking from one woman to the other, stunned. "That lady ... that was her? That was Leena Mishra?"

Gargi saw red. "What do you know about Leena Mishra, huh?" she snarled at him. What business did he have talking to them about Leena-di? She itched to give Surya a resounding slap.

Surya, suddenly serious, looked her straight in the eye.

"I know that Leena Mishra's husband is dead."

A stunned silence enveloped the reception area. Had there been anyone there apart from the three of them, they would, perhaps, have been stunned too.

After several seconds of utter shock, Gargi was finally able to find her voice. "Dead?" she said, her voice hoarse. "You're saying Ritesh Mishra is dead? Are you out of your mind?"

"I am not," said Surya, "but Leena is."

Gargi could not believe what she was hearing. A fog was enveloping her brain.

How did Surya know that Ritesh sir was dead?

And if he was … what was Leena doing?

What on earth was Leena doing?

Surya's voice broke through the haze in Gargi's brain. Ritesh had been dead for nearly seven months.

Around the time when Leena had stopped coming to the salon.

Apparently he had suffered a major heart attack a year ago. ("Thankfully it was mild," Leena had said.) He was bedridden for a while, before he fell victim to a stroke and passed away in hospital.

Leena was at home when Ritesh died in the ICU.

"How … how do you know all this, Surya?" Gargi choked, tears streaming down her face.

Surya looked at her, longing to take her in his arms and comfort her, but knowing that was a bad idea. "I also do deliveries at their gated complex," he said, quietly. "I heard it all from the staff and security personnel there. All the residents there know what is going on."

"What … what is going on?" Even Riya's voice was quavering. "What did you hear?"

Surya took a deep breath. "That Leena Mishra lives in complete denial of her husband's passing. Every day, she dresses up for him, and stays indoors. No one is allowed to enter her house, except their maid, who goes there once a day to clean and cook." Surya paused, wondering if he should continue.

"And?" Gargi pushed, her heart pounding.

"Leena Mishra talks to her maid as though Ritesh Mishra is still alive," he said. "Food is cooked for two every day, even though most of it goes to waste. His clothes are washed, ironed and laid out every day, as though he will wear them."

He stopped, and then looked at Gargi. "The only time Leena Mishra leaves her house," he said softly, "is to come to the salon."

Gargi did not know what to do with all this information. Riya was staring at her, a mix of fear and sorrow on her face. Surya's eyes were, for once, not on her, but on the ground.

Her own brain was racing.

Ritesh sir was dead.

He had been dead for months.

He had had a major heart attack.

Six months.

Those six months…

Leena had disappeared right after Ritesh's death.

And three days ago, she had returned.

Talking about starting a family with Ritesh. A baby. Chinese food. Pasta.

Today she spent the whole day with Gargi, getting ready for her anniversary. Talking about roses. Romantic messages. An anniversary-night celebration...

"I can't wait to go back home. I can't wait for Ritesh to come home."

Leena's words. They reverberated in Gargi's ears.

"Talking to you gives me peace."

Gargi froze.

At 11 a.m. sharp the next morning, the bell atop the door of the salon tinkled.

Gargi smiled. She was here.

"Gargi!" Leena, with her radiant beauty, walked right past a stunned Riya, and made a beeline for her favourite masseuse. "Oh gosh, I have so much to tell you!" Gargi watched as her eyes softened. "Last night was so wonderful," she said. "Your dada loved the perfume so much! I have to tell you everything he planned for me!"

She looked around, then back at Gargi. "I came straight here this morning," she said, something catching in her throat. "All I could think was, I can't wait to tell Gargi everything!"

Gargi tried hard to fight back tears as Leena reached out to clasp her hands. "Thank you for being there for me," she said. "I've always needed a friend like you."

Gargi smiled at her softly, then gestured her towards the spa room. "It's all ready for you, Leena-di," she said. "I'm here to listen to you."

4

ACROSS THE RIVER

By the time the Sanyals reached their platform, Sonali was already showing visible signs of annoyance. It was a hot and humid afternoon at Howrah Junction, and the jostling crowds were beginning to get to her. It did not help that her husband, Abir, seemed unperturbed; as she wiped a bead of sweat off her brow, his calm demeanour irked her even more.

Once they reached their platform, Sonali decided to focus her attention on other things in order to keep herself from snapping at her husband. So irritated was she that she did not even pause to think *why* she was so annoyed. The platform was alive with the cacophony of vendors peddling cha and snacks to weary travellers. The couple stood among the teeming hundreds, both of them bearing a suitcase and packets of food, waiting expectantly for their train – the Saraighat Express, which would take them to Guwahati. Abir Sanyal, a tall and bespectacled man with a warm smile, glanced at his beautiful wife, not missing the fact that her piercing brown eyes held a mix of longing and frustration.

"It's happening, Sona," Abir said, his voice filled with excitement. "We are finally going there!" His enthusiasm was unsurprising; after all, he had meticulously planned this trip for months. It was the first time they were going somewhere together in nearly five years. It's remarkable, thought Abir to himself ... quite remarkable how time and the flush of youth slip away when each day is a clone of the last – a constant stream of bickering, of losing themselves. He viewed this trip as a second honeymoon for Sonali and himself, a chance to rekindle their love. A chance to mend, to heal. To begin afresh.

They sorely needed this time together, and he knew it.

Sonali, on the other hand, did not seem as enthused as her husband. As the train pulled into the station, she did not even break out into a smile when Abir turned to her and said, "I have a surprise for you."

"What?" she asked, her brow furrowing. "What is it?"

He could not miss the ever-so-slight flicker of suspicion in Sonali's eyes when he told her that he had booked an entire coupe on the train for the two of them, so that they could spend the whole journey together, undisturbed. He could not avoid the sharp stab of pain as his heart broke a little. As Sonali's lips curved into a disapproving frown, he realized that his wife did not think he could do anything nice for her.

"A coupe?" she scoffed. "Please, Abir; you booked the coupe so that *you* could travel in peace and quiet. We both know you did not do it for me." A shadow of some phantom emotion – pain? – flitted across her face before disappearing. She was not done yet. "Besides, you forgot my shawl. I told you a hundred times to pick it up before leaving the house. Don't you know how cold it gets in an AC coupe?

You clearly never think about these things – especially if they concern me!"

Abir's eyes softened. "I'm sorry, my love," he said, quietly. "I forgot. I'll find a way to keep you warm. I promise."

"Don't bother," snapped Sonali, as they heaved their luggage onto the train, and then climbed on themselves. "I'll make do with the blankets." She turned her face away from Abir and strode towards their coupe, hardening her expression to hide how she was feeling inside. This journey would be difficult enough as it is; it would not do to cry. She swiftly wiped a tear away as they entered their coupe and set down their belongings.

This journey, after all, meant different things to her and to Abir, she thought. Going to Kamakhya, the renowned temple known for its mystical fertility blessings, was supposed to be a sacred pilgrimage for those who wanted to have a child – something that Sonali had yearned for over several years. But she was also acutely aware of the fact that the trip itself was a symbol of her failure – her failure to become a mother, to produce a child.

The pilgrimage to the Kamakhya temple was the Sanyals' last, desperate attempt – a plea to the Almighty to fulfil their desire to have a child of their own.

If this, too, failed, they would have to consider adoption. But Sonali knew, in her heart of hearts, that that's not what she wanted.

Abir understood Sonali's pain, but had always believed their love could overcome any obstacle. To Sonali, however, Abir's optimism and look-on-the-bright-side attitude felt like an insult, a trivialization of her pain, of the gaping void she felt within her heart.

She yearned for her husband's support and understanding, but felt like she could never get it.

Abir wanted nothing more than to support his beloved wife; she just never seemed to see it.

Perhaps, he thought, with hope in his heart, *this trip might change that*.

The Saraighat Express had pulled out of Howrah Junction; the rumbling sounds of the wheels sped up, and the train's gentle undulations became a steady rhythm as it moved towards Bardhaman Junction. As they settled in, Sonali's irritation seemed unrelenting. She berated Abir for everything, from the coupe's harsh lighting to the stiffness of the seat and the freezing temperatures.

Each complaint was like a dagger piercing Abir's heart. But all he wanted to do was to reach out and soothe his wife's grief. With a smile on his face, he unwrapped the food packet he was carrying. It was time for some refreshments, he thought. This would cheer Sonali up.

Sonali felt a wave of joy when she saw her favourite snacks emerging from the packet. Abir had remembered that she enjoyed munching on *chanachur* during train journeys! "*Ei nao* (Here you go)," said Abir, placing the packets on the foldable table between the two of them. "*Tomar pochhonder mukhorochak ami enechhi.* All your favourite savoury snacks."

Sonali was about to reach out for the newest flavour of her preferred *chanachur* brand with glee – but something struck her, and she swiftly withdrew her hand. Her eyes flashed with anger. "What is all this?" she demanded. "Do you want me to fall sick? You know how unhealthy and overly spicy all of this is."

Stunned, Abir tried to pacify her. "*Achha thik achhe, tumi chinta koro na.* Don't worry. I'll have them," he said.

"What?" she exclaimed. "You can't! It's not good for you either!" She swiftly took the packets from his hands and put them into her bag. Abir could not help but grin; he had caught a glimpse of his wife's childlike, caring heart – the heart of one who enjoyed eating packaged snacks, and also worried about her husband's health.

He then noticed Sonali rummaging in her own packet of food – and watched in wonder as she set out plates for the two of them and served up his favourite comfort meal, *luchi* and *deemer dalna*. "You made this for me?" he asked, looking at Sonali tenderly.

Caught off guard, Sonali tried to appear nonchalant. "*Aar noy toh ki*? What else did you expect?" she barked. "These are the only items I could bring that would not turn stale immediately. Kindly eat fast, so that I can clear up!" Abir, still touched that his wife had cooked his favourite items and brought them along for the ride, reached for her hand.

But Sonali pulled away, anger overcoming her face again. "I'm not in the mood for jokes!" she shouted. "Please finish eating fast, the compartment is beginning to smell of the *deemer* curry!" Abir pulled back, subdued, and finished the rest of his meal in silence.

It had been a couple of hours, and they had spent most of the time not talking to each other. As Abir looked at his wife, staring forlorn out the window of the moving train, he longed for conversation with her. There used to be a time when they could talk about anything with each other. Where had that Sonali gone?

Hearing the rustle of a packet, Sonali turned towards her husband, and watched him bring out a box of sweets. Her heart leapt with joy – she had a massive sweet tooth. But her combative instincts took over again as Abir opened the box. "Why have you brought so many sweets?" she demanded. "Don't you remember your last blood sugar reports? You're not supposed to be eating any of this!"

Abir chuckled. "*Achha baba*, don't get angry. *Ami shudhu ektai khabo*. I'll eat just one."

"*Na*! *Tumi ektao khabe na*! Not even one! Give me the packet." Sonali reached across the table and snatched the box away. Then she settled into her seat, picked out a *kheer kodombo*, and started nibbling on it, her face lighting up with childlike pleasure.

Abir's heart sang to watch his wife enjoying herself. "Do you know, my love," he said, quietly, "Ma picked out those sweets for me to carry for the train journey, since she knows you like them so much."

He regretted his words almost immediately. It was as if thunderclouds had rolled into their coupe. Sonali froze, dropped the half-eaten sweet back into the box, and stood up, her body trembling with rage. "Your mother knows we are going to Kamakhya?" she said, her voice quavering. "Did you tell her about our *manot*? Did you?"

Abir scrambled for words, taken aback by this outpouring of anger. "I … yes, I did," he stammered. "She was concerned about you … and she is hopeful that you will get what you want from this visit…"

"I knew it!" Sonali was seething. "You could not even keep this one thing to yourself, could you? Your mother has *never* lost an opportunity to make snide remarks about my infertility, and now it seems like you bear a grudge against me too!"

Abir stood up. "Sona, you know that's not true," he said, his voice even. "Ma loves you, and has never said anything of the sort to you. She is always thinking about how she can ease your suffering. She would never do or say anything to hurt you, and neither would I! Why can't you see that?"

"Shut up, Abir!" screamed Sonali, tears streaming down her face now. "I even overhead her calling me *baaj* once!" Turning away, she sobbed inconsolably. "Your mother and you hate me because I can't give you a child. Admit it!"

At that moment, something in Abir snapped. He stood up, rage filling up his entire being. "Maybe your life would be easier if you stopped complaining so much and behaving like a victim all the time!" he roared. "Always angry, always dissatisfied, always, *always* picking on me! Nothing I do pleases you, *nothing*! You're unbearable!"

As he uttered these words, heaving with rage, he noted the shock in his wife's eyes, swiftly replaced by deep hurt. But, by now, he was beyond caring. He had had enough.

The argument raged on, punctuated by the clatter of the train as it began to pass over a river. Those travelling via rail along that route would often be advised to look out over the breath-taking beauty of that river, which lasted for about twelve minutes of the journey. But the Sanyals were locked in their fight. Anyone passing by outside the coupe would have been able to hear every word, but Abir and Sonali were oblivious to the world outside their little cocoon of bitterness, including the spectacle of the swirling river.

They were still yelling at each other when there was a knock on the door of their compartment. Yanked out of their ugly fight, Sonali, deeply embarrassed, quickly wiped away her tears. Abir composed himself, then said, "Come in!"

A young man in a crisp Indian Railways uniform entered the coupe. The Sanyals noted that he was the ticket checker, an unexpected and unwanted guest in the midst of their heated exchange.

"What's going on here?" the young man asked, a hint of concern in his voice. "Is everything alright?"

Sonali was momentarily taken aback, but soon resented the insinuation. "That's none of your business," she said icily. "We're just having a little disagreement. Would you like to see our tickets?"

The ticket checker looked at them with a knowing smile. "Disagreements can turn into big problems if you let them fester. Sometimes, it helps to talk things out."

Neither Abir nor Sonali knew how to react to such unsolicited advice from a stranger. But something about this young man, who appeared to be in his mid-twenties, with kind eyes and an oddly calming presence, helped quieten their anger. Abir, ever the optimist, nodded in agreement with the man's words. "You're right," he said. "We should calm down and talk."

The ticket checker looked at the two of them for a second. Then he looked straight at Sonali. "Didi, do you mind if I sit down for a few minutes?"

Sonali was rendered speechless for a second; she had not anticipated the tug on the heart she felt upon being called 'didi'. The last time she had heard that was from the mouth of her beloved little sister, Rupa, whom she had not seen in years.

"Yes, do sit down," she said, much to Abir's surprise. "Would you like a glass of water?"

"Sure, thank you." The young ticket checker smiled. "My name is Anirban, by the way."

"I would like to say something, didi, if you don't mind," said Anirban, as he took a sip of the water.

Sonali looked at him with caution. "You may," she replied. "*Bolo*?"

Anirban's soft eyes moved from Sonali to Abir, and then back to Sonali, before dropping to his lap. "The two of you must really love each other."

Sonali was about to let out a loud sneer, before the look on Anirban's face stopped her. It was almost … wistful. She snuck a glance at her husband, to gauge his reaction to Anirban's words. Abir, whose handsome face was always an open book, bore the same look of curiosity that Sonali felt.

"Why … why do you say that, Anirban?" Sonali asked. She was genuinely puzzled. This young boy had, after all, walked in on a screaming match. Wasn't it obvious to him that there was something wrong?

Almost as if he had read her mind, Anirban looked directly at her, and, much to her surprise, let out a loud chuckle. "Did you hear yourselves?" he said. "Only two people who love each other deeply would be invested enough to fight like that."

Sonali and Abir both froze, suddenly uncomfortable. What on earth was this young boy, this stranger whom they had invited to sit with them, saying?

And why did his words hit so close to home?

Abir's thoughts were racing. Anirban was implying – nay, clearly saying – that Sonali still loved him. *But if that is true*, he thought, *why is it not evident? Why was she always finding fault with him, making him feel helpless*?

Sonali, for her part, felt her anger rising. Love? Was this young boy suggesting Abir loved her? The same man who blamed her for her infertility? The same man who had just called her 'unbearable'?

"Why would you say that?" she demanded, her eyes flashing at Anirban.

"Before I answer that, let me ask you something," responded Anirban, without missing a beat. "What were you fighting about?"

Sonali's eyes widened, and she was about to give Anirban a talking-to, before she was interrupted by the young boy. "Didi, you do not need to tell me if you don't want to," he said, quietly. "But if you do, I could help. At the very least, you'll feel lighter."

Sonali considered his words, pain suddenly clutching at her heart. How could she articulate the problem? How could she explain to Anirban that at the crux of the conflict with her husband was their childlessness?

She did not have to; Abir, who was silent all this while, spoke up.

"Sonali ... can't have children," Abir said, his voice catching in his throat. His words tore through Sonali's heart. *I was right all along*, she thought, *close to tears ... he hates me because I cannot be a mother. He hates me...*

"...but she just does not seem to understand that I love her more than anything else in the world! And that nothing is more important to me than her happiness! I try, in every way I can, to show her that … but I seem to fail every time!"

Abir's words broke through Sonali's inner monologue. She stared at him. What was he saying?

Anirban jumped in. "And you, didi?" he asked gently. "Do you believe him? What, according to you, is the problem?"

Sonali found herself at a loss for words. Her heart was pounding and breaking at the same time … she did not know how to answer without breaking down.

So she did. Sonali wept and wept. She did not understand, she just did not understand. Abir, in his entire life, had never uttered an untruth. And yet, he was sitting here, telling this young stranger that he did not care whether she could give him a child or not, as long as he had her by his side.

Did he mean it? Could it be true?

"Didi?" Anirban asked again. "Talk to me, please."

Sonali took a deep breath, wiped her eyes, and looked at the young man. "I … I feel so worthless," she said, her voice quavering. "All I ever wanted was a child with Abir; it's been my greatest desire, and" – she stole a glance at her husband – "I have always known he would be a great father."

Abir looked at his wife, unable to believe what he was hearing. His heart contorted with guilt and grief to hear Sonali, the light of his life, say that she felt worthless.

Did she not know that she was worth a thousand suns to him?

Anirban leaned forward, his dark eyes fixed on the Sanyals. "Didi, Abir-da, what the two of you are going through is deeply painful," he said quietly. "It is challenging and emotional for any couple. You could both agree on that, right?"

Sonali and Abir nodded, forlorn.

"But perhaps there is one more thing on which you both can agree," Anirban pressed on.

"What is that?" asked Abir, puzzled.

"That the two of you are each other's worlds."

Silence ensued. Neither Sonali nor Abir knew how to respond to that – yet, both desperately wanted it to be true.

"Abir-da, neither you nor I can quite understand the depth of didi's grief, even though you can feel a lot of it," said Anirban, looking at Abir directly. "This is where your love comes in. She needs your patience and understanding even in her hardest moments, even when she may not seem agreeable. It is especially in *those* moments that it's crucial for you to reassure her that you love her no matter what … and, most importantly, that you don't blame her, not even for a second, for something that is beyond her control."

Abir nodded, his eyes filled with love and sadness. "She knows I love her, more than anything in the world. I just wish she could see that."

"Maybe you need to keep showing her that, through kindness … even when you think it's hard to be kind," said Anirban, gently.

While his words sank into Abir's mind, Anirban turned his attention back to Sonali. "Didi, you do see that Abir-da loves you deeply, don't you?"

Sonali looked at Abir, her eyes brimming over. At long last, she nodded. "I know. He's always trying to show me that he does. I just could not see it."

Anirban reached out and took her hands in his. "Didi, this is a challenge that you both face together; not something that you blame each other for."

Sonali brushed away her tears and looked at Anirban. "But what do I do with all this guilt, Anirban?" she asked, her voice laced with desperate grief. "I feel like I'm holding Abir back from having the family he's always wanted."

Anirban smiled softly. His next words shook Sonali to the core. "Didi, *you're* the family he's always wanted." The young boy paused. "Without you, his family does not exist."

With those words, it was as if a switch had flipped in Sonali's brain. With trepidation, she stole a glance at her husband, hoping he would meet her gaze with the same love she felt in her heart for him at the moment. Abir was looking at her too, and, when their eyes met, he held out his arms to her.

With a sigh of relief, Sonali let her husband envelop her in his warm, loving embrace. She then looked up at him. "You really don't mind if we cannot have a child?" she asked, a tad fearfully.

Abir looked down at her tenderly. "What do you think, my love?" he asked. "Do you think I would want for anything in my life if I have you?"

Seeing the two lovers reunite thus, Anirban's face broke into a beaming smile. "Besides, didi," he interjected, "your love for each other is what truly matters, whether or not your family expands." He stared out at the river, his eyes suddenly faraway. "No matter what happens, as long as you both have each other, your lives will be full."

Sonali and Abir looked at him with a mix of awe, embarrassment and gratitude in their eyes. "Thank you, Anirban," said Abir. "Thank you for bringing my Sonali back to me."

Anirban smiled. "Abir-da, misunderstandings are common in all relationships, but more so when a couple is dealing with something as emotionally charged as this," he said, softly. "The key is to support each other through the tough times."

His eyes went back to the river outside the window, soon about to go out of sight. "Never say anything unkind. It may become impossible to heal from that. No matter what your visit to the holy temple brings, know that you'll be happy as long as you have each other."

With a proverbial boulder lifted off their hearts, the Sanyals laughed, cried and embraced, oblivious to the fact that even though they were Guwahati-bound, neither of them had mentioned their pilgrimage to the Kamakhya Temple to Anirban.

Abir wiped away a tear as Anirban stood up to leave. "Anirban, I cannot thank you enough," he said. "You are a stranger we met barely twenty minutes ago; but in that time, you helped us see the error of our ways!"

"Stranger? He is no stranger," interjected Sonali, with a smile on her face. "He called me didi; he is family now." She turned to the young man. "Anirban, when you are done with your rounds, will you come back and have dinner with us?"

Anirban, now standing at the other end of the coupe, smiled warmly. "Of course, didi," he said. "Thank you for the invitation." He paused for a second, his eyes on the window. "We've crossed the river," he said, almost wistfully. "You missed the view."

"We'll look out for it on our way back from Guwahati," said Abir. "Come back soon for dinner! We'll be waiting."

"Alright." Anirban headed out of the door. Right before exiting, he paused, and turned around. "Love is a precious gift," he said, looking at both Sonali and Abir. "And it's rare to find a kindred soul who values you above all else. Don't let hurtful words take that away from you. No matter how bad things are, never ever let them go past the point of no return."

With that, he disappeared.

With newfound love and understanding, Abir and Sonali chatted merrily over the next few hours, barely registering the passage of time. It was only when Sonali looked out of the window that she realized that night had fallen. A minute later, there was a knock on their coupe door, and their dinner was delivered to them.

"Abir, it's late!" she exclaimed. "It's past nine. Anirban should have been here by now."

"You're right," said Abir. "I do not think we should start eating without him, but the food will get cold." He paused, then came to a decision. "Let's wait for ten minutes," he said. "I'm sure he'll be here soon."

Ten minutes passed, then twenty; Sonali and Abir ate their dinner in silence, crestfallen that Anirban had not shown up. "He's probably busy," ventured Abir, seeing Sonali's sad face. "He is on duty, after all."

But a second later, there was a knock on the door. Sonali's face brightened. "That must be him!" she said. "Dinner's over, but he can have some dessert with us. Come in!" she called out.

The door opened, but it was not Anirban who entered. It was an older man, also in a ticket checker's uniform. Abir and Sonali looked at each other, puzzled. Hadn't Anirban already checked their tickets?

"Sir, there seems to have been some mistake," said Abir to the elderly ticket checker. "Our tickets were checked a few hours ago by someone else. I can show them to you, if you like."

Something unreadable passed, like a shadow, across the older man's face. He took off his spectacles, pulled out a handkerchief, and wiped his eyes. Then he said, softly, "You met Anirban, didn't you?"

"Yes!" said the Sanyals in unison. "He was supposed to come back and have dinner with us," continued Sonali. "But he did not show up. Is he still on his rounds?"

The old man did not answer immediately. He turned around, sat down, and asked for a glass of water.

And then he spoke.

"Seven years ago, a tragedy occurred on this train," said the elderly man, his face grave. "Anirban was aboard, travelling with his wife. They were going on their honeymoon." Abir looked at Sonali, puzzled, then looked back at the ticket checker.

"The same Anirban we met? He then became a ticket checker? What a coincidence!"

"Well, it *is* a coincidence, of sorts," said the old man, with a wry, almost sad smile on his face. "But not in the way you think."

Sonali felt a little jab of fear in her heart at the old man's sad smile. "What happened?" she asked, clasping Abir's hand.

"On this very train, on that journey, Anirban had a huge fight with his wife, whom he loved dearly. It was a tragic misunderstanding; something about her being unable to have a child. I was the ticket checker then; I remember hearing the fight. *Prochur kotha katakati hoyechhilo*. A lot of ugly words were exchanged." He paused, as though unable to continue. Then he looked at the Sanyals.

"Deeply wounded by her husband's words, Anirban's wife jumped from the moving train into the river we crossed a few hours ago. Anirban, unable to bear the grief, jumped out after her."

He looked out of the window, into the darkness, unable to meet the Sanyals' gaze.

Abir and Sonali sat in stunned silence for almost five minutes, gaping at the ticket checker. It was Sonali who spoke first. "So … the person we saw … the young boy who called me didi…"

The old man nodded. "Anirban's spirit now roams this train. Sometimes he appears as a ticket superintendent, sometimes as a dinner delivery boy … always trying to prevent warring couples from making the same mistake he did."

He looked up. "Pardon my intrusion, but if he appeared to you, I can only assume that he was trying to save your relationship."

"How do you know that?" asked Abir.

"When did Anirban come here?" asked the older man. "Think carefully."

Sonali and Abir looked at each other with a mixture of horror and awe. Abir spoke first. "We were fighting. Anirban knocked on our door … just when the train was going over the river."

The ticket checker smiled. "Fear not. He was here to help. He saw the love in your hearts, and wanted to save you from a path of bitterness from which there is no going back."

He got up, opened the door, and, like Anirban, turned around one last time.

"Congratulations on your love," he said quietly. "And thank Anirban."

With that, he left, closing the compartment door behind him.

5

ALL FOR LOVE

It was a typical Sunday afternoon in 1995 in the heart of south Calcutta – the neighbourhoods were quiet, almost soporific, as families, caught in a post-lunch stupor, succumbed one by one to their afternoon siestas. The street corner ice cream carts were stationary, their guardians sprawled atop them in deep sleep. A lifeless afternoon breeze soughed through the tree-lined streets, augmenting the absence of any bird call.

It was on one such afternoon, in the quiet haze of her living room in a two-bedroom apartment on the eighth floor of a building complex in a corner of Golf Green that Shyamoli Banik told her son, Soumya, that she had found the perfect girl for him.

Soumyadeep Banik was the pride and joy of Shyamoli and Bimal Banik. This was not just because Soumya was their only child – it was also because he was a bright student, top of his class almost every year.

This was just as well; after all, Bimal and Shyamoli had worked tooth and nail to get him admitted into a school of great repute. They left no stone unturned to ensure he flourished academically. Bimal worked hard at his job as a senior manager at a bank, and Shyamoli, a teacher, gave tuitions after school hours to supplement the household income. It was soon after marriage, in 1967, that they moved into their Golf Green home, their hearts filled with hope for the future, and Soumya on the way.

And when, two months later, she had held her newborn in her arms, looking down at his cherubic face and tiny hands, Shyamoli had vowed that Soumya would never want for anything.

My son, she decided, *would get whatever he wanted*.

Of course, in the 1960s and 1970s, children were supposed to want for themselves what their parents wanted for them. So Soumya, naturally, wanted academic excellence – and Shyamoli made sure nothing got in the way of that. Bimal curried favour for years with the higher-ups at his workplace to secure a place for Soumya at an expensive school. The quiet boy could read by the time he was three; when he joined school, his parents decided that his days of play were over. For Soumya, after-school hours were spent studying while the other children in the building complex played outside; by the time he was giving end-of-year examinations, he would stay awake all night studying, Shyamoli by his side, keeping vigil.

She would take him to school, and wait in the playground's seating area with other, similarly motivated mothers, waiting for Soumya to finish. When he emerged, she would have his tiffin – a sandwich, a banana, biscuits and juice – ready for him. His nutritional needs were foremost for her, for they would augment his classroom performance.

And Soumya did not disappoint his parents. He shone at school, always at the top of his class, with a few awards for extracurriculars like debating and chess thrown in for good measure. He was a teacher's delight – quiet, diligent, brilliant. "His test papers are a joy to behold," Shyamoli would hear at every parent–teacher meeting. "And he is a well-mannered boy. He will do very well in his life." It was music to her ears.

Once a month, to celebrate Soumya's unwavering performances at school, the family would go out for dinner. These outings were the highlights of Soumya's month. His parents and his books were his entire world.

He had no friends. Shyamoli had decided he did not need any. *My son*, she thought, *cannot get distracted*.

Her strategy ensured that Soumya excelled all the way through college – he became a gold medallist in economics at Calcutta University, before securing a good job at the city office of an FMCG company. Once there, Soumya went from strength to strength. By his twenty-eighth birthday, he was already in the running for the post of assistant vice-president, and had given his parents an all-expenses paid holiday to Port Blair.

Shyamoli was elated. Soumya was her pride and joy.

So she decided that it was time he had a wife. He was twenty-eight, and soon to get a massive promotion and salary hike.

The time was right.

So Shyamoli set about looking for a bride for her son.

And, after months of scouring matrimonial columns, considering proposals brought forth by relatives, and consulting the family astrologer, Shyamoli's prayers were answered.

She had found Titli.

Titli Ganguly was an orphan. Her parents had died in a freak bus accident when she was six years old.

In the wake of this tragedy, Titli was taken in by her father's younger brother, Shishir. He entrusted Titli to the care of his sister Malati, who lived with her brother and sister-in-law Deepa. All three adults treated the bereaved child with a lot of love, but it was Malati who took the most care of her. Under her *kaka*, *kakima* and *pishi*'s watchful eyes, Titli gradually felt the ache of her parents' absence begin to dull.

By the time she was fifteen, she barely remembered them.

In her kaka's ancient, dilapidated north Calcutta house, Titli grew up amidst much laughter, spending long afternoons playing gaily in the house's adjoining field. Her cousin, Sankhayan – Shishir and Deepa's son – was just two years older than her, so the children grew up like siblings.

Sankhayan was the light of Titli's life. The feeling, however, was not really reciprocated by him.

But it did not start like that. At the beginning, Sankhayan helped his pishi take care of Titli – he oversaw her lessons, helped her with her homework, and protected her from the neighbourhood bullies who lost no chance to pick on the orphaned child.

But as Titli grew older, she took on the mantle of caring for her family. This displeased Sankhayan, who was getting a degree in pharmacology and chemistry, and had hoped his sister would study, become a doctor, and make something of herself. Titli, however, was content with being at home, learning how to cook, and caring for her loved ones.

Her elders, of course, approved of this. ("The way to your future husband and mother-in-law's hearts will be through their stomachs," Deepa teased her. "*Bhalo kore ranna ta shekh*!") But Sankhayan did not; his opinion about his younger cousin plummeted, and soon bordered on disdain. When he was offered a plum position in a fast-growing pharmaceuticals company in Bangalore, he grabbed it with both hands; he no longer wanted to live at home with Titli. In his eyes, she was unambitious and unpolished – an embarrassment to him.

But Titli's love for Sankhayan never waned. When he packed his bags and left, she felt like she had lost a parent all over again.

She was not one to complain, of course. Titli never complained to anyone, about anything.

But her loneliness after Sankhayan's departure was not lost on the elders.

Titli was twenty-six. Their hearts ached to see her so forlorn.

It's time, they decided. It's time to find her good husband.

Their enquiries began.

And, a few weeks later, Deepa received a call from a relative, who taught at a well-known Calcutta school. Her colleague, a certain Shyamoli Banik, who lived in Golf Green, was looking for a suitable bride for her only son.

"*Khoob bhalo chhele*," said the caller. "Tall, fair, handsome. Good family. *Bhalo chakri kore*. He would be perfect for Titli."

Her eyes shining, Deepa hung up the phone and rushed to Malati's room.

A week later, when the elders informed Titli that her wedding had been fixed, the young woman did the only thing she always did when she felt alone and fearful. She called her dada.

Her calls to Sankhayan were usually met with irritation. She did not blame him; he was a very busy man. Thankfully, this time, upon hearing the news she bore, Sankhayan's tone took on a degree of warmth she had not heard in a long time. "*Tor biye*?" he exclaimed, his voice coming through clearly over the phone.

"Yes, dada," Titli said, her voice small. "I don't know what to do…"

"It will be alright," interjected Sankhayan, in a rare show of support. "You know Ma and Pishi will never choose someone who is not the best for you."

"But ... *tui thakbi toh, dada*?" Titli's voice quavered over the phone. "I can't do this unless you are there!"

There was a pause at the other end, in the span of which Titli could feel her heart drop. *He won't come*, she thought. *Dada ashbe na*.

"I'll be there." Sankhayan's voice rang out over the line after what felt like an eternity. "*Chinta korish na*."

Despite herself, Titli laughed out loud.

In her heart of hearts, she knew that Sankhayan was probably glad that she was going to get married and go away.

But it didn't matter. She could stomach that, if it meant her dada would at least be by her side at the wedding.

She wiped her tears, bid her brother goodbye, and hung up.

Soumya stared at his mother in horror, his plans of an afternoon siesta vanishing.

"What did you say, Ma?"

Shyamoli looked at her son's face, anticipating what was coming. She steeled herself.

"I've found a wonderful girl for you, *shona amar*," she said, her voice taking on a placating tone. "*Onek toh boysh holo*. You're old enough. It's time you settled down."

Soumya could not believe his ears. Was his mother really suggesting he get married?

"Ma, what is this?!" Soumya could feel his anger rising. "You did not even ask me!" His rage unsettled him. He was not used to raising his voice, especially while speaking to his mother.

Shyamoli knew this too. Decades of managing every aspect of her son's life had taught her exactly how to gauge his reactions to everything, right down to the tiniest detail.

She knew what worked.

So she looked him straight in the eye.

"Do I have to consult you when I am the one who knows what is best for you?" she said, her voice quiet and steely. She watched as her son's demeanour changed at the sound of her tone.

"*Na*, Ma, you don't," said Soumya, his eyes cast down, his voice barely a whisper.

Shyamoli changed tack. "Babu, I'm also growing old," she said, quietly, watching the guilt gradually shadowing her son's face. "I long to see you settled; I long for a daughter-in-law, a girl I can love and treat as my own daughter." She paused, then looked pointedly at Soumya. "I long for a grandchild."

She took her son's hand, ignoring the fact that his pulse was racing. "Can't you do this much for your old mother?" she asked, gently. "I promise you, you'll love the girl. Her name is Titli." She stopped, her eyes shining, thinking about the sweet girl who had shyly served her tea and *singaras* at her north Calcutta residence just a week ago. "She is perfect."

Soumya was silent for a long time, his eyes far away.

What is he thinking? wondered Shyamoli, a little kernel of worry entering her heart. Soumya had never disobeyed her in his life.

Would this be the first time?

But then, he looked up at his mother's worried face. His eyes softened.

"*Thik achhe*, Ma," he said quietly. "You know I would do anything for you." He paused, his face brightening. "Tell me about Titli."

Eleven months later, amid a lot of fanfare, and with her family of four by her side, Titli married Soumyadeep.

It took Titli no time to fall in love with her husband. Soumya doted on her. He was kind, caring, attentive, and showered her with affection. Most importantly, he treated her family as his own. The elders could not stop gushing about him. He was the son-in-law of their dreams – respectful, humble, and mindful of their beloved niece's happiness.

Sankhayan took a little longer. He met Soumyadeep for the first time at the wedding itself, and initially displayed scepticism. But he soon warmed up to his new brother-in-law, and they became friends.

Nothing could have made Titli happier. For one, it meant that she, too, would get a chance to spend more time with her brother. Moreover, it had not escaped her notice that her husband lacked friends, and lived mostly under the thumb of his strong-willed mother.

Titli did love her mother-in-law. Shyamoli had given the newly-weds the best possible wedding gift – a separate flat in the same building in Golf Green, rented in their names. ("I want you both to have your own space, but also stay close to us.") But Titli knew that what Shyamoli really hoped for was the best of both worlds – a chance to relax, encumbrance-free, in her own house, while also having her daughter-in-law close by to cook for and take care of her.

Titli did not mind. How could she, when she had no reason to complain? She had a loving husband, nice in-laws, and a brother who had taken a transfer back to Calcutta so that he could keep an eye on his ageing parents and aunt, now that Titli no longer lived with them.

In fact, with Sankhayan back in the city, Titli was elated. Their relationship seemed to be improving; he came over regularly and spent time with her while Soumya was at office. Sometimes, the three of them would hang out after Soumya came home from work. But she did meet with a fleeting shade of hostility and resistance the few times she tentatively broached the subject of their childhoods. All she wanted to do was talk about old times, but Sankhayan was not willing – it seemed to remind him of his disappointment in her and disdain for her life choices.

Eventually she stopped, but realized there was another way she could feel closer to her brother.

She cooked for him. He loved to eat what she cooked.

"Don't eat so many *luchis,* dada!" she once lovingly chided him. "They're not good for you."

"Uffff! Be quiet and fry me a few more," retorted Sankhayan. "Once you are done, you have to make Soumya's parathas!"

Titli grunted in exasperation. It was not easy to make luchis and parathas separately to suit both her cousin's and husband's tastes! But she could not complain; seeing them well-fed made her happy.

And happy she was. In fact, she was exceedingly grateful for Sankhayan's presence. For one, he seemed to have a way with elders; every time her mother-in-law called on the landline, Sankhayan, if he was around, answered the phone, and then proceeded to jabber with the old woman for ages. This afforded Titli – who would, otherwise, have to cater to Shyamoli's whims – some much-needed respite. Moreover, her dada was the only person she knew who made the effort to draw her reclusive husband out of his shell.

Her dear, sweet husband. Titli smiled, looking forward to Soumya's return from office. Almost every day, he brought back something for her. The other day, it was a sari she had once spotted in a shop window and said she really liked. He had remembered, and bought it for her as a surprise. Then, yesterday, it was a surprise visit to the cinema, a rare treat for someone like her, who had never entered a cinema hall before marriage.

She treasured these gestures even more because she was aware that they were not common. After all, she had been taught not to expect too much from her husband; it was *her* job to keep *him* happy. And yet, here was Soumya, never saying too many words, but showing his love in his own way – through warmth, hugs and gifts.

Hers was an idyllic life. She truly had everything she wanted.

That is, until she fell sick.

⁂

It started with a niggling stomach ache that would not go away – mild at first, then sharper and sharper as the days went by.

Titli, who never complained, kept it under wraps. She was certain it would go away with a few painkillers.

Except that it didn't.

One day, while serving Soumya his lunch, a razor-sharp stab of pain made Titli cry out and double over.

Soumya, his face overcome with terror, kneeled over her. "*Ki hoyechhe, shona*?" he asked anxiously, slowly making Titli sit up. "Are you okay?"

"It's nothing," groaned Titli, trying to regain her composure. "Just a bit of pain in my stomach."

"What? Since when?" Soumya demanded. Titli looked her husband in the eyes, unable to lie to him.

"For … a week or so," she said, grimacing.

"A whole week?" Soumya's eyes flashed with anger. "Why did you not tell me? We are going to the doctor immediately."

Before Titli could protest, Soumya had bundled her into his car, and sped off.

After a thorough examination, the family doctor concluded that it was nothing to be alarmed about – it was a slightly severe case of gastritis that would go away with medication. "And, of course," he said, looking at both Soumya and Titli, "please ensure you switch to an anti-inflammatory diet. Cut down on fried food."

Soumya, looking relieved, helped his wife back into the car. But on the drive home, Titli noted his face darkening. "What happened, my love?" she asked. "You look upset."

Soumya turned to look at her briefly. "I feel both guilty and angry," he said.

"Why?" asked Titli, puzzled.

Soumya sighed. "Guilty, because you are forced to eat the unhealthy food that I ask you to make for me all the time," he said. "And angry at your brother! He works in pharma. He knows so much about health and medicine. He should know better than to expect you to cook and eat so many luchis every other day!"

Titli was speechless. She had never heard anyone say a word against her dada before.

"But … Soumya…" her words trailed off.

"I don't want to hear anything, Titli," Soumya said. "From now on, no parathas, no luchis, no deep-fried food at home. We'll eat rice and vegetables." He glanced at his wife. "And by 'we', I mean all of us. Including your brother. And that is final."

Titli kept quiet. The rest of the drive home passed in silence.

When they reached home, Soumya's mother and Sankhayan were already waiting in their living room. Titli had messaged both of them ahead of time. As Shyamoli fussed over Titli, Sankhayan asked Soumya what had happened.

"What do you think happened?" snapped Soumya, his eyes flashing at his brother-in-law. "She's developed gastritis thanks to all the fried food she has to make for you and then eat herself all the time!"

Sankhayan stared daggers at his sister's husband. "Are you actually blaming me for this?" he growled. "You're her husband! Don't you know that gastritis runs in our family? And isn't it *your* job to keep an eye on her health?"

"Soumya! Dada! Please stop!" pleaded Titli, weakly, deeply distressed at this shouting match. "I am alright! The pain has subsided." She turned to her mother-in-law for support. But, for once, Shyamoli was at a loss for words. She had never seen Soumya get so angry.

Titli, realizing that Shyamoli would not say anything, turned back to Sankhayan. "Dada, I think you should go home now," she said, quietly. "Come see me tomorrow. I promise I am alright now."

Sankhayan gave her a withering look, and, without a word, walked out the door.

Titli, of course, was not alright.

The pain would just not go away.

She did not know what to do. The agony was growing day by day.

But she knew one thing. There was no way she could let Soumya know.

She had never seen him so angry before. If he found out she was in pain again, he would go ballistic.

If she went to a doctor, Soumya would find out. And she could not let that happen.

So Titli did the only thing she knew to do when she was in distress. She called her brother.

"Dada, I've had a niggling headache for a few days, and the Crocin is not working," she lied, hoping against hope that Sankhayan would not detect the slight quaver in her voice. "Do you think you could get me something stronger from your office? I don't have the time to go to the pharmacy right now." She paused, then gulped. Titli was not used to telling lies.

"Why do you need something from my office?" asked Sankhayan, his voice sounding a tad suspicious. Titli's heart began to pound. Would her brother catch her in a lie?

"Whom else will I ask, dada?" she said, trying her best to sound flippant. "You literally work in a pharmaceutical company. You would know what would be safe for me to take."

Sankhayan was silent for a second, as if he were thinking about her request. "Okay," he said. "I'll get you something mild. Have you told Soumya?"

"It's just a headache, dada," Titli said, trying to sound irritated. "No need to make such a big deal out of it!"

"Don't talk to me like that!" Sankhayan's sharp tone made Titli cower on the other end. But he seemed to realize how harsh he sounded, for his voice immediately became more apologetic. "Sorry for snapping," he said. "Go take a nap. I'll see you in the evening." He paused. "If you're better by then, we could all go to the park."

Titli smiled. "Sure, dada," she said. "I would love that."

In the weeks that followed, Titli's pains only worsened. She began to develop heartburn as well. The painkillers were not working; she would need something stronger.

Unfortunately, there was no way she could ask her brother for stronger medication. He would smell a rat immediately. Titli did not want to think about what might happen then.

So she kept taking only the medicines that her brother got for her, sometimes popping two or three at a time in the desperate hope that an increased dosage would dull the pain. Sankhayan, too, looked puzzled every time she asked him to replenish her stock.

"Didn't I just bring you two full tabs last week?" he asked. "Why do you need more so soon?"

"I've misplaced that set, dada," she said, turning away and busying herself with something in the kitchen so that Sankhayan would not detect the guilt writ large on her face. "*Ene de na*, please. In fact, get me something a bit more ... fast-working, if you can."

She waited for his response, her heart in her throat.

Eventually, Sankhayan spoke. "Do your in-laws know about this?"

Fear bubbled through Titli's veins. Her first instinct was to lie, but she knew Sankhayan would soon find out the truth if she did. She had no choice.

"No, they don't, dada," she said, hesitatingly. "But that's only because this is nothing!" she rushed to add. "They would create a mountain out of a molehill, and Soumya's already got so much on his plate at work. You know he tends to worry too much, even when there's nothing to worry about!"

A dreadful pause ensued, during which Titli felt like Sankhayan would immediately guess what was going on.

But he did not seem to catch on. "Okay," came the reply. "That makes sense. But make sure you don't overdo it. I'll bring you something stronger tomorrow."

Titli could feel the relief coursing through her veins, amidst the pain.

As Sankhayan was getting up to leave, Titli turned to him. "Dada," she said hesitatingly. "Why don't you come stay here with me for a few days?"

Sankhayan looked at her, puzzled. "Why?" he asked, his brow furrowing. "Are Soumya and you fighting?"

"No no, dada, nothing like that!" Titli rushed to reassure him. "Everything is fine. It's just that … having you around makes me happy. This family feels complete. *Tui toh emni tei ashte thakish.* You eat half your meals here. It would be nice if you came and stayed with me every now and then." She paused. "Like old times."

Sankhayan was looking at his sister, and Titli braced herself for that familiar look of hostility on his face every time she mentioned their childhoods.

But, much to her disbelief and delight, Sankhayan actually looked visibly happy with the idea. "Whatever my kid sister wants," he said. (Was that a slight hint of affection she detected in his voice?) "You might as well let Soumya know that he can expect a permanent *kebab mein haddi* situation soon!"

In a rare gesture, he ruffled Titli's hair, and was soon out of the door.

A minute later, Titli doubled over with pain.

This went on for eight more months. Eight long, agonizing months. Till, one day, Titli, while getting into the car with Soumya and Sankhayan, collapsed on the road.

The next thing she knew, she was in a hospital bed, her mind foggy, a battery of tests being run on her. Through the haze of sedatives, she could make out the blurry outlines of her family members at the foot of her bed. Her pishi, kaka, kakima. Her parents-in-law. Soumya. Her dada.

Two days later, the reports were in.

Titli had a ruptured gallbladder, and Stage 4 stomach cancer.

"Beta, you were in pain for months," the family doctor and the specialists said. "Why didn't you say anything?"

Titli did not respond. She just wanted to sleep.

"Her bloodwork is a mess," the doctors told Soumya. "It shows that she's been taking copious amounts of medication that we were not aware of. Possibly to numb the pain. But they only aggravated her gallbladder rupture. Someone should have monitored her intake."

"What … what are her chances, doctor?" Sankhayan asked, desperately, guilt writ large all over his face.

"Palliative care is the only option at this point, I'm afraid. She has about three to four months to live."

A pall of gloom settled over the Banik household in Golf Green the day Titli came home from hospital. Soumya was beside himself with grief. Shyamoli, trying not to cry in front of her sick daughter-in-law, told her that he had been making frenzied calls to specialists in New York and London. Sankhayan, she said, had been poring over her reports and speaking to his colleagues, trying to find out if there were any new treatments or clinical trials that Titli might be eligible for.

He had been walking around with a lost, haunted look in his eyes, said Shyamoli.

When Titli finally got into bed, longing for rest, Soumya came into the room. Wordlessly, he curled up next to his wife, enveloping her in a hug. Through her half-asleep, exhausted state, Titli could feel his silent tears, soaking through the fabric of her kameez.

Grief and exhaustion mingled in her heart like a drug. She wanted to comfort him, but before she could, she fell fast asleep.

Over the next three months, as Titli rapidly lost weight and hair and found herself increasingly confined to a wheelchair, her family amped up efforts to cheer her up.

Soumya celebrated her birthday with aplomb. Shyamoli, Malati and Deepa cooked her favourite food items, using as little oil as possible. Sankhayan, who had moved into the guest bedroom in Titli's flat, arranged for an exclusive screening of a new Shah Rukh Khan movie at a local cinema hall that his colleague's family owned.

Even in her weak state, Titli was elated. She could feel how deeply loved she was.

As she sat in the cinema hall, booked out especially for her, watching *Pardes* with her husband and dada sitting on either side of her, she took both their hands in hers.

The two people she loved most in the world.

Later that night, as Soumya helped her get into bed, she looked up at him, her eyes filled with guilt and sorrow.

Looking into her eyes, Soumya broke down. Scooping his frail wife up in his arms, he wept and wept, for what seemed like hours. "You'll fall sick if you cry so much, my love," Titli whispered, holding him as his sobs slowly subsided.

"I can't lose you." Soumya choked out, slowly releasing Titli's body and taking her hands in his. "I wish I could have done better by you. I wish I had more time."

Titli touched his face with her soft hands. "My love," she said, looking straight into his eyes, "these last three months have been the happiest of my life. I only wish..." Her voice faltered, just for a second, "... I only wish I had a lifetime more to love you."

Gathering his wife in his arms, Soumya lay down. Soon, both of them drifted off to sleep.

The next morning, Titli was gone.

It was just another Sunday afternoon in the heart of south Calcutta – the neighbourhoods quiet, a lifeless afternoon breeze whispering through the tree-lined streets, augmenting the absence of any bird call.

Back home after cremating his wife, Soumya walked into the bedroom he had shared with Titli. Tracing the shape of the wood on their four-poster bed, he felt the death grip of grief encircle his heart again.

He had left his parents and Titli's family outside to deal with the visitors. He had come into this room for a moment's respite. Just for one moment of peace.

But was there any peace to be had? Soumya sat down on the bed, on Titli's side. He stared out of the window.

He was still lost in his thoughts when he felt Sankhayan's arms encircling him from behind. Hugging him.

Lacing his fingers through Sankhayan's, Soumya tilted his head back, resting it on his lover's.

Silently, he wept, as Sankhayan held him.

He did not see the haunted look of guilt flashing in Sankhayan's eyes.

SANKHAYAN

I remember our first meeting. At Titli's wedding.

My eyes locking with his, and the world standing still. For both of us.

Soumya. My soulmate.

Our growing bond. Our secret, inner world.

All the evenings spent together.

Our deepening, passionate love.

And our burgeoning grief. The grief of having no future together.

And, with that, a burgeoning anger towards what – who – stood in the way.

Titli.

I remember that feeling well.

My sister. I had held so much hope for her. So much hope! I wanted her to do well in life! But she turned out to be an embarrassment to me. An embarrassment to my entire family.

And now, here she was, getting in the way of my first and only chance at happiness.

Everybody in the world thinks that people like Soumya and me are freaks.

Simply because of who we love.

We cannot even choose who to love openly. But here was Titli, getting to marry and live with Soumya – simply because society accepted it.

She did not deserve Soumya.

Soumya, the love of my life.

There were so many nights that the two of us held each other and cried, while Titli slept! So many nights wondering how we could possibly get through life like this. Pretending, every single day!

And I could not even tell Soumya how much I resented Titli. Soumya is a good, pure soul; I could tell he was very fond of his wife.

It made my heart burn with anger. The fact that I could not even hold his hand in broad daylight, but she could have him, all to herself, day and night … day and night…

I could not bear the thought! The thought of her touching him … can't you see how that would break my heart?

I was desperate.

But then…

Titli's stomach ache.

The first sign that something was wrong.

The first sign of hope.

A possibility that it could get worse.

Could it get worse? Could it … be made to get worse?

I could never forget how Soumya had spoken to me the day Titli first went to the doctor.

That tone. From my lover, because of that girl.

If anyone was in my place, it would make their blood boil too.

I had to find a way to keep her away from Soumya. But how could I do it without him finding out?

Soon enough, the first chance presented itself.

The phone call from Titli.

Because, when in distress, Titli would have done the only thing she knew to do.

She would have called me. Her brother.

Headache, my foot, I had thought. My sister was a terrible liar. I knew right off the bat that it was more serious than that.

This was my only chance. It was my only chance to create some distance between Titli and Soumya, and it was handed to me on a platter.

The medicines could start.

A steady, never-ending stream.

Straight from the office.

Supplied to her in secret.

She would, after all, never tell Soumya what she was doing.

Clueless Titli. Making my job so much easier.

Month on month of unmonitored medication. Strong, unapproved medication.

Until…

This was not what I had wanted.

I had not anticipated this.

All I had aimed for – all I had wanted – was for the medication to make her weak. Weak enough that she would be too tired to touch Soumya.

That is all I had wanted. For there to be distance between her and my love.

I did not want her to die.

I hated her, but I did not want her to die.

And yet, I killed her.

It was me.

I didn't mean to. I was desperate.

All I wanted was to be close to Soumya.

And I thought…

I thought this was the only way.

6

MOTHER

June 2021

It had only been twenty minutes since Medha Gaekwad had reached the funeral, and she could already sense that something was not right.

She was met with shifty eyes on masked faces the moment she arrived. Even before she could go and give her condolences to the deceased's closest kin, she had been shunted to an empty chair at a corner of the room, and asked to sit down. No one had come to speak to her after that.

Most onlookers would have interpreted this as normal social distancing in a world that was still recovering from Covid, but Medha knew better. And she wasn't surprised. Sriram had warned her that this would happen, even though he was the one who had told her to go.

But no, that wasn't what seemed wrong. Medha could not quite put a finger on it, but she had been in the crime branch of the Mumbai police long enough to sense that something was amiss, anywhere, if it was.

And something was definitely wrong here.

Medha observed the handful of people milling around, the grieving family members, the wails, the silences. The deceased man was Vishnu Venkataraman – her father-in-law's brother, and Sriram's own uncle. ("He struggled with cancer for many years," Sriram had said. "It's no wonder that Covid finally struck him down – his already weakened body could not withstand the onslaught of the virus.") A large, garlanded picture of the handsome man occupied pride of place in the room. Around it, bouquets of flowers were piling up, and the light of numerous diyas were flickering while a priest chanted mantras. But Medha's eyes were drawn to Mr Venkataraman's family – *my family, too*, she thought, absent-mindedly – as they remained immersed in their grief.

Lalitha, Vishnu's wife, clad in white, bore a faraway look in her eyes, briefly coming back to the present moment every now and then to acknowledge a greeting or a condolence by a visitor. Next to her sat Anush, her son, crying his eyes out on her lap while their aged family helper rhythmically stroked his back. Even though Anush was twenty-three years old, at that moment, Medha thought, he looked like a frail, forlorn child of twelve. Surrounding them were other, peripheral family members – among whom Medha had not been invited to sit.

It had already been three years since her marriage to Sriram, but his conservative Tamil family still could not come to terms with the fact that their beloved boy had married a Maharashtrian – that too a policewoman five years older than him.

And so, in her three years of being Sriram's legally wedded wife, Medha had never been to a Venkataraman family get-together. This was the first time that she was officially attending an occasion as a part of the family.

She briefly pondered the irony of the situation. Here she was, among her husband's family, and yet, she could not even sit with them.

But her instincts had always been sharper than her emotions, and her thoughts soon turned back to the niggling sensation that something felt off. Her eyes scanned the room, taking in every person, every masked face, trying to find a landing point for her uneasy feeling.

Unable to do so, she finally got up to leave.

Locking eyes with Lalitha, Medha briefly bowed her head. Lalitha looked at her for a second, as if trying to place who she was. When recognition dawned, she looked away.

Sighing, Medha tried to catch Anush's eyes. But the poor man still had his face buried in his mother's lap. It was futile. Even the helper, stroking his back and urging him to sit up, could not get him to move.

Medha gave up, and headed out of the door. But with every step, her sense of unease increased.

Looking back, she took a silent vow to figure out what was wrong.

"I'm telling you, Sri, something was really, really off," Medha said. She had returned from the funeral an hour ago, showered, changed, and got ready to go to work, much to her husband's chagrin.

"Medha, it's your day off," Sriram said. "I don't understand what you are doing. We had decided to spend the day together!"

Medha turned around to look at her gorgeous husband. Even with his injured foot – the reason he could not attend the funeral – the sight of him, half undressed and lounging about in their bed, tempted her for a second to get out of her uniform and climb into the sheets with him.

But she couldn't shake her uneasy feeling. And unless she did something about it, she knew she would not be able to rest.

"I need to do this, Sri," she said, tying her bootstraps. "There's something very wrong in that house."

"This is what being in the crime branch day in and day out does to you," grumbled Sriram. "You end up looking for problems where there aren't any."

"That's not what this is," said Medha, quietly. As much as Sriram loved her, she knew he would not understand.

"What is it that you suspect?" asked Sriram, the irritation apparent in his voice. "You think he was murdered? There was nothing suspicious in his medical reports!"

"I know," said Medha. "But I still need to look. At motive, for instance. Your uncle was an extremely wealthy man; his wife and son would immediately inherit everything upon his death—"

"Medha, have you lost your mind?" Sriram was getting visibly angry. "Anush is a good kid, no matter what his troubles have been. And are you seriously suggesting that my aunt could be capable of murder? She is the nicest, kindest person you could ever meet! On top of that, she's a highly respected public personality. She has spent her life helping orphaned children through her NGO. Does that sound like a murderer to you?"

"I did not say anything of the sort," Medha said, now on the verge of losing her cool.

"But you implied it," Sriram snapped. Then, he looked at his wife's face, and his eyes softened. He held out his hand to her. Without a word, Medha took it, and sat down next to him.

"Look, you know how hard it's been to get them to accept us," Sriram said, gently stroking his wife's warm hand. "It took us three years to even get an invitation to visit them, and when we did, it was an occasion of mourning." He looked anxiously at Medha's beautiful face. "I really want a return to normalcy. My parents don't live here anymore; Vishnu *Chitthha* and his family were my only family in Mumbai till I met you. I really want everyone I love to get along … even though Chitthha is now gone." He looked up at her, his eyes shining with tears. "Chhittha was the pride of our family. Please don't try to sully his family's name, Medha. It will destroy all our chances of being happy."

Seeing the grief in Sriram's eyes made Medha's heart ache. She gently touched his cheek. "I don't want to cause any damage to anyone, my love," she said. "But please, Sri, I implore you … try to understand where I'm coming from." She took his hand and placed it on her heart. "You know the kind of person I am; you know I can't rest until I find out the truth about something. You chose this; you chose me."

She curled her fingers around his.

"Please let me do this. I promise that if I don't find anything in one month, I'll drop this and never speak of it again."

Sriram looked into his wife's eyes, and sighed. His stubborn, annoying, beautiful Medha.

"Alright, fine," he finally said. "One month."

"One month. It's a deal." Medha smiled, gave her husband a long, lingering kiss. "Thanks for trusting me, Sri."

"When you look at me like that, it tells me everything I need to know," said her husband, leaning in for another kiss.

But before he could get it, Medha looked like lightning had hit her. She jumped out of bed, grabbed her things and raced out of the door, leaving a mystified Sriram scratching his head.

It took her almost exactly a month to find out what was happening. Her investigation, owing to its unofficial nature, was harder than she anticipated it would be. But she figured it out.

It shook her to the core.

May 2000

Vishnu Venkataraman entered his house at seven o'clock on a Monday morning, sleep-deprived but in high spirits. After a gruelling week of travel and meetings, he had finally come back to Mumbai in time for a weekend of rest, relaxation and passionate lovemaking with Tanisha.

The high was short-lived. His mood soured the moment he spotted his wife, Lalitha, emerging from the bedroom they had not shared in years. As she approached him, her eyes filled with both questions and knowing, all he could focus on was her body – short, rotund, rolls of fat visible underneath the drape of her sari, a far cry from the svelte figure she had possessed at the time of their wedding.

It angered him. And when he thought of Tanisha's delicious body, which he would have to wait another whole week to savour, it angered him even more.

All he felt when he looked at Lalitha was revulsion. The woman loved to eat, and did not care two hoots about her figure.

She had stopped caring right after her second miscarriage, and piled on the weight soon after. Weight that she never lost again. Who would believe she was only thirty-five? The thought that his wife had lost two pregnancies did not linger for long in Vishnu's mind.

He could not even divorce her, no matter how much he wanted to. If it had been up to him, Lalitha would have been out of his life by now, and Tanisha would have been his bride. And yet, "Do *not* divorce Lalitha under *any* circumstances!" had been the refrain he had heard from his friends and colleagues for years. Their reason? They were a "power couple" in the corporate and development sectors of Mumbai. Lalitha was as big a name in the nonprofit world as he was in the corporate world; leaving her would not be to his benefit.

"Have all the affairs you want, bed every woman you want. But make sure you go home to Lalitha." The words of his best friend, Ronnie. Words he had lived by for over a decade. Words he was living by even now, on the brink of forty.

But Ronnie had also said another thing to him.

He had told him to have a child with Lalitha. "It doesn't matter if you can't have one biologically," he had said. "Adopt one."

A child would be great for his career, his brand, his image, his professional prospects, Ronnie had said. More so if it were adopted. "It's cool to adopt," Ronnie had said. "Looks good to the world. You are the CEO of one of India's biggest MNCs. Your wife is a high-achieving NGO founder. Can you imagine how great it would look if you gave an orphan or an abandoned child a home?"

Vishnu was pulled out of his thoughts by Lalitha tapping him on his shoulder. The interruption made him glare down at his wife. Unfazed, she looked right back at him.

"How was your trip? I heard you got back on Friday."

"I did."

"It's Monday today."

Vishnu looked at his wife, irritation writ large on his face.

The hag knew everything. About Tanisha, about his "business trips", about his history of infidelity. She knew where he had been over the weekend. She had always known, and had never really created a fuss. It was a "don't ask, don't tell" system that worked for them – for him, at least.

"I know what day of the week it is," he snapped. "Am I going to get a cup of coffee or not?"

Lalitha gestured to the drawing-room table. "It's there, waiting for you. Raju just made it."

As Vishnu turned to walk towards his morning refreshment, Lalitha pulled on his arm to stop him. "Vishnu," she said, her quiet voice sounding serious. "The papers are there on the table, next to your coffee. You need to go through them carefully." Her grip on his arm tightened. "We are only a few steps away. Don't mess this up, please."

With that, Lalitha released his arm, and disappeared into another wing of their vast Mumbai home.

Vishnu sat down, took a long, slow sip of his filter coffee, and began to leaf through the folder his wife had left for him.

As he looked through the minutiae carefully, he could not help breaking out into a smile.

Everything seemed to be airtight and in order. Lalitha had made sure of that.

The woman, for all her faults, was more competent than anyone he knew, Vishnu thought. It didn't hurt that she had worked with shelters, rescues and India's nodal adoption agency for over a decade.

As Vishnu set down the adoption papers and finished his coffee in another long sip, he smiled again to himself.

Very soon – within a year, perhaps – he and Lalitha were going to be parents to a little boy.

The kid would keep Lalitha occupied. He would be able to have even less to do with her than he did now.

He would be able to stay over more often with Tanisha. Lalitha wanted this child so much, she probably would not even notice his absence.

The thought filled Vishnu with a buoyant joy.

And anyway, Ronnie was right. It's cool to adopt. It will look good to the world.

Eight months later, with all legal formalities completed, little Anush became a part of the Venkataraman family. Vishnu and Lalitha threw a massive party to celebrate their new three-year-old.

Little Anush, whose life had begun in an orphanage in Pune, had finally come home to where he belonged.

The newspapers and TV channels went mad, and the who's who of Mumbai rejoiced with them.

June 2002

Things, of course, did not go according to how Vishnu had envisioned it.

The arrival of Anush in their lives *did* evoke great admiration for him in his professional and social circles. He could not deny that.

But he had banked on Lalitha doing the lion's share (actually, all) of the child-rearing. What he had not bargained for was her refusal to give up working.

Lalitha was a career woman through and through. Her work took her outside Mumbai on a regular basis, sometimes for two weeks at a stretch.

In her absence, she expected Anush's other parent to do his job and pick up the slack.

Vishnu, of course, was not willing to do that. So what if he was Anush's father? The day-to-day responsibility of being a parent is not what he had signed up for.

And so, the last two years had passed in a frenzy of rotating nannies and anxiety-riddled work trips for Lalitha. When Anush was about to turn four, Lalitha, in her desperation for reliable help, even moved her own, aged mother into her house, just so that there would be one other person with whom she could leave Anush when she travelled.

Tragedy struck when, in January of 2002, her mother passed away. The next few months were spent in intense mourning and worry for Lalitha, who had to deal with her grief and a growing toddler at the same time.

It was in June that she saw a ray of hope, when her friend from another block in the same luxury apartment complex told her about a woman who had been looking for full-time work for a while. "She hails from Kolhapur," Rashi said. "She's been working part-time at Neha's place, and Neha has vouched for her. These Marathi women are good with children. She also really needs the money – she apparently has ailing parents back in Kolhapur. Interested in meeting her?"

Lalitha was very interested. "Send her to me tomorrow?"

The interview went swimmingly – Anush took to the woman, Lalitha liked her, and three weeks later, after serving her notice period at Neha Balachandran's house, Prajakta Kolte joined the Venkataraman residence as Anush's full-time nanny. She learnt everything about Anush's schedule, and offered to do a whole bunch of other household chores as well. Anush called her Tai, and, for some reason, so did Lalitha. It did not matter that they were almost the same age – there was a comfort to calling her Tai that Lalitha really enjoyed.

For the first time in two years, she rediscovered what it felt like to sleep through the night.

August 2012

"God knows what I was thinking! The kid is a bloody liability!" Vishnu yelled. He picked up the glass he had been drinking from and smashed it onto the floor, as a terrified Lalitha looked on and Anush cowered in the corner.

Two bombs had been dropped on the Venkataramans at one go. One was Anush's report card for his Class IX final exams – he had failed in most of his subjects. The other was a final, medical confirmation from Anush's doctors about something that Lalitha had suspected for a long time – that her son was dyslexic.

"Vishnu! What are you doing?" shrieked Lalitha. "Your son is right here!"

"I DO NOT CARE!" roared her husband, causing Tai to scurry away just as she was inching towards the shards of glass on the floor to clean them up. "No wonder he is such a good-for-nothing! Can't get good grades, can't do anything right … I spend lakhs every year sending him to the most expensive school in the city, and what do we have to show for it, huh?"

"Vishnu, he is … he is good at other things," said Lalitha, desperately trying to calm her drunk husband down. *He should not be drinking*, she thought, in the middle of her racing thoughts. *His cancer's only just gone into remission.*

"Oh really? What else is he good at, my dear?" Vishnu snarled. "Wasting time on his phone? Hanging out with his friends? Is he going to make a career out of any of these things?"

"You know he's good at sports! And … and he takes a real interest in the work I do at the NGO, so he could always volunteer and learn the ropes—"

"Lalitha, your son is useless!" Vishnu bellowed, interrupting her. "You have spo—"

"HE IS YOUR SON TOO, VISHNU!"

Vishnu was momentarily stunned at the force of Lalitha's scream. She had never, ever spoken to him like that. As he stomped off to pour himself another whiskey, his wife standing desolate in the middle of the living room, Vishnu did not notice his son, crushed to the core, slink away to the kitchen.

Ten minutes later, Lalitha found him there, having cried himself to sleep in Tai's arms. For a few seconds, the two women exchanged a glance, as if to say, *he does not deserve this*.

Then, Lalitha gently took Anush to his bedroom to tuck him in, while Tai went to sweep up the broken glass.

April 2018

"I've made arrangements for Anush to move."

Lalitha nearly choked on her morning coffee. "Wh-what?"

Vishnu glanced up at her from his phone and glared at his wife. He did not like having to repeat himself.

"Anush is going to move to my old Chembur flat. He's twenty-one, and does nothing. It's time he started fending for himself."

"Fending for himself? What do you mean? His entire life is here, at home, with us!"

"And *that* is the problem!" Vishnu snapped, sitting up in his chair. "You and his ayah are his entire life. You both have spoiled him rotten, and he lives off me, thinking that daddy dearest will always bail him out of all of life's problems. Well, no more." He stood up. "Anush is the son of a self-made man. We grew up with modest means, and I never took a penny from my father beyond the age of eighteen. Everything I am today, I have built on my own. Can your son say that for himself?"

"But ... Vishnu..."

"There will be no arguments about this," Vishnu said, the calm in his voice chilling Lalitha to the bone. "My decision is final."

"What will he do for his meals? His essentials, his needs..."

"He will have to figure that out for himself," Vishnu said flatly. "We will pay for his groceries, but he will have to cook his own meals, and no extra money will be given to him. It's enough that he's getting an entire flat to stay in for free. Surely he can figure the rest out by himself."

"Saab, if I may..."

Vishnu turned to look at Anush's nanny. "What is it, Tai?"

"No, nothing ... I was ... just going to say..." The small woman, already frail for her age, was quaking with fear. "I ... was just going to say ... please don't send baba away, saab..."

The look of murderous anger in Vishnu's eyes was almost enough to send her scurrying away, but she persisted. "If you send him away, I ... I'll be out of a job..."

"Why? Why will you be out of a job?" Vishnu asked. "He is an adult! You are not his nanny anymore, you are a worker in this house. You'll take care of Lalitha and me."

"But, Vishnu," Lalitha interjected, desperately. "He is our son, and he is supposed to take care of us, na? Look at how well he tended to me last year when I broke my leg..."

"Lalitha, it's final." Vishnu stood up, ready to go out. "I am retired, and cannot take one more second of that idle layabout in my house. Either he learns to fend for himself in the old flat, or..." Vishnu paused for just a second, so that his next words would have the desired impact on his wife, "... your darling son can kiss his inheritance goodbye."

With that, he strode out of the door.

Lalitha and Tai stood there, looking at each other helplessly.

June 2019–April 2020

Vishnu kept his word. He shunted Anush out of their luxurious Mumbai flat and into a much smaller apartment in a far more modest part of town.

Naturally, Anush struggled. Anyone would, when thrown into the deep end of the pool after having grown up in the lap of luxury; but Anush struggled more than most. After all, he had almost no skills. His learning disabilities and his father's neglect had ensured that.

Grief and anger bubbled up inside him in a toxic cocktail, day in and day out. Whatever money his mother and his Tai managed to funnel to him secretly, he would promptly go and spend on buying ganja.

By the time 2020 came around, he fell into bad company, smoking up in street corners at odd hours of the day and night, waking up in shady parts of town and not knowing how he got there.

Through it all, he hated his father. Hated him with a vengeance.

And then, one day, a plague that was sweeping across the world found its way to India. In March, the country shut down.

In April, Anush's mother called.

She was sobbing so hard he could barely hear what she was saying.

"Your … your father's tested positive."

Anush could not make out the rest of what Lalitha said as the phone dropped from his hand.

July 2020

It was with great trepidation that Anush rang the bell to his childhood home – the inside of which he had not seen in a year.

When his Tai opened the door, Anush burst into tears. After clumsily disinfecting his hands with the sanitizer she held out, he flung himself into her arms, disregarding all rules of social distancing. For a minute, the two of them wept.

Through the haze of his tears, in the far corner, he could make out the hunched silhouette of a woman, sitting quietly at the drawing-room table.

His mother. Lalitha.

Pulling himself out of Tai's embrace, he raced towards his mother. "Amma!" he sobbed, as he got close to her. "Amma!"

"A-Anush?" Lalitha looked up, her eyes shining with tears. "You came?"

Anush stopped in his tracks. Even though she was masked, Anush could see how gaunt his mother's beautiful face had become. Throwing all caution to the winds, he went and sat at her feet.

"Amma, are you also ill?"

Lalitha looked at her son tenderly, taking in his thin face and pallid colour with mounting pain in her heart. "No, darling, I am, by God's grace, alright. So is Tai. Only your … father got it." Her voice lowered when she mentioned Vishnu.

"Is he … in his room?" Anush asked, trying and failing to keep the bitterness out of his voice.

Even though she had not seen her son for a year, she could tell he hated his father.

"Yes, he is," replied Lalitha. "Do you want to go see him?"

She watched as the darkness rapidly settled on her son's features. "Not after what he did, Amma," whispered. "Not after what he did."

"Sweetheart, he has been really ill," implored Lalitha, longing to reach out and touch her son's face, but fearing it at the same time. "I'm sure he will be happy to see you..."

"No I won't." That old, familiar, sneering voice rang out through the massive drawing room, as mother and son both stopped talking. His heart pounding, Anush turned around slowly – to see his father slowly hobbling out of his bedroom with the help of a walking stick.

Even though the illness had made him weak, the venom in his eyes remained intact.

"Once a good-for-nothing, always a good-for-nothing," barked Vishnu, the force of his words making his entire body shake. "Turning up here in the middle of a bloody pandemic! Do you have any concern for your mother's or your Tai's health?"

"Vishnu ... he, he came to see you..." Lalitha's voice quavered.

"NO, I DID NOT!" Anush's bellow reverberated through the room, shocking everyone into silence. Tears running down his face, he stood up, and faced his father head on. "I ... *I wish you had died*! I wish the bloody virus had taken you!"

In the deathly silence that followed, the only sound was of Anush's wracking sobs as he raced past his father and Tai, and ran out of the door.

After what seemed like an eternity to Lalitha, Vishnu slowly turned to face her. "When things open up properly, call the lawyers," he said. His voice was raspy with weakness, but laden with steel. "It's time to do what I should have done long ago."

As he hobbled back into his room, Lalitha's blood ran cold. She knew what he meant.

May 2021

But Vishnu never did get the chance to amend his will.

When the Delta virus hit, it hit him hard.

His body, already weakened from the first wave and the recurrent cancer treatments, struggled to withstand the second onslaught.

On 29 May 2021, Anush's phone rang.

It was Tai.

"Baba … your fa … saab is in the ICU," her frail voice quavered on the other end of the line. "He … we ensured he stayed at home, that no one could come into contact with him. But … we don't know how…" Tai broke down. "I'm sorry, baba. I'm so sorry."

Choking back the tears and the bile rising in his throat, Anush steadied his voice. "Tai, take care of Amma," he said. "Keep me updated."

"Okay, baba. Are you alri…"

He hung up before she could finish.

Two days later, the call came.

Vishnu Venkataraman was dead.

June 2021

It had been a week since Anush had moved back home with his mother. The funeral was in two days' time.

There was so much to be done that he was losing his mind.

And yet, no amount of frustration could dilute his joy at being back home with his mother again.

"Amma, thank you," Anush said, as they sat eating lunch together while Tai served them hot idlis. He could not help but notice how much his mother had wasted away over the past two years.

The thought made him angry ... not just at his father, but also at Tai. His father had been an awful human being. But couldn't Tai have taken better care of her?

"For what, darling?" Amma asked, putting a morsel of food into her mouth.

"For always standing up to him for me," he said. "He was horrible to you, but you still fought for me, every time."

Lalitha's eyes clouded over with sadness as she reached out to clutch her son's hand. Lost in their thoughts, mother and son barely noticed Tai ladling sambhar into their bowls.

What Anush did notice, however, was how fragile his mother's hand felt in his. The realization hit him like a tonne of bricks. Amma's hand was skeletal!

"Tai, why is Amma in this state?" he snapped. The suddenness of his anger made both the women jump. "Have you seen her hands? The bones are sticking out!"

"But ... baba..." Tai started, but Anush was having none of it.

"I left my mother in your care," he said, his eyes flashing. "You've seen what my father was like; you should have taken care of her, ensured she ate well and stayed healthy. I ... I feel like asking you to leave now."

Anush got up and stormed into his room. The cruelty of his words hung in the air. His food remained untouched.

Tears streaming down her face, Tai started clearing up his plate.

"Tai…" said Lalitha, her voice small, "don't pay any heed to his words, he is just tired."

"I know, Memsaab." Tai laughed, wiping her face vigorously. "Baba would not hurt me. He is a very good man. He is a very good man."

As she watched Tai walk back to the kitchen, Lalitha could have sworn she was still crying.

July 2021

Three weeks had passed since the funeral. And even though it would take years for the ghost of Vishnu Venkataraman to be exorcized from the house, Anush could finally, for the first time in his living memory, feel his mind and body relax.

But he was still worried about his mother. Lalitha was happy to have her son back, but the loss of her husband seemed to be hitting her really hard. She hardly talked, kept forgetting where she had put her things, and wanted to sleep most of the time.

Anush and Tai did their best to bring her back to a semblance of good health. Anush ordered the healthiest of ingredients, and Tai cooked nutritious meals with them. She made hot beverages twice a day for Lalitha, and Anush took her for walks around their apartment complex.

And still, Lalitha's health continued to deteriorate.

In fact, she may have died within a month of her husband's funeral had a certain Medha Gaekwad not showed up.

When she did, she walked into the house, took Lalitha's cup of tea out of Tai's hands, handed it over to her subordinate, and arrested Tai.

MEDHA

My name is Medha Gaekwad, and I am a criminal investigator with the Mumbai Police crime branch.

A couple of months ago, I attended the funeral of Vishnu Venkataraman, my husband's uncle. Sriram, my husband, could not go, so I went for both of us.

From the get-go, I could sense that something was not right.

I couldn't tell what it was at first, naturally. Of course things would seem off, some would say; you are entering a space of grief and loss. What can feel right about that?

But to me, it felt like something more. Like something else was amiss.

So I tried, for the hour that I was there, to put a finger on it. I couldn't. I looked at everyone, the family members, the guests. Their faces were masked, so I observed their voices, their words, their eyes.

Their eyes.

Later that day, Sriram said something to me. "When you look at me like that, it tells me everything I need to know."

It tells me everything I need to know.

That was it. That's when it hit me.

Because, when I left the funeral, I had locked eyes with Lalitha Venkataraman. Her eyes were faraway, absent, grief-stricken, almost empty.

It's all I had paid attention to in that minute, when what I should have been focusing on was the gaze of the person sitting behind her.

Prajakta Kolte.

Tai.

Stroking Anush's back, but looking at Lalitha.

Looking at her with singular jealousy, bordering on hatred.

I had seen it. But I had paid no heed.

How many of us pay attention to the help? Even as a policewoman, I had missed it. I am not proud of that.

But now that I had put my finger on it … I had to get to work.

And so I started digging, unsure about what I would find. I didn't even know if I wanted to find it; I just knew I needed to.

That look of hatred. It had to lead somewhere.

It did.

Everything I am about to tell you, everything that my investigation yielded, has already been documented in Prajakta Kolte's confession.

Two hours ago, she confessed to having orchestrated the death of Vishnu Venkataraman. To having attempted to murder Lalitha Venkataraman.

And to being Anush Venkataraman's biological mother.

Prajakta Kolte from Kolhapur, whose husband died, leaving her pregnant, with no money, and no way to take care of herself or her old and ailing parents.

She travelled to Pune in desperation with her new-born in her arms, leaving him outside the gates of a police station, hoping against hope that he would survive.

She then found a job in a biscuit packaging factory. The income helped her make ends meet and send money back to her parents, but did nothing to assuage the yearning she felt to be close to her child.

Prajakta's supervisor, a certain Swati Kirkire, noticed her suffering. Starved for conversation and a listening ear, Prajakta decided to trust the elderly lady, and told her everything.

Mrs Kirkire, through her networks, found out that the child, after being discovered outside the police station and being sent to the hospital for medical tests, had been placed in Pune's Loving Hearts Orphanage.

When I was taking Mrs Kirkire's statement, she told me that she had hoped Prajakta would have found peace in knowing that her son was safe in the orphanage.

But that, apparently, was not enough.

Now that she knew where he was, she wanted to be close to him.

She begged, cried, and pleaded. Eventually, Mrs Kirkire relented.

Orphanages do not allow workers who do not have a trusted history of volunteer work. So there was no way in which Mrs Kirkire could have got Prajakta a job or even a volunteer role at the orphanage without greasing several palms.

She did, however, manage to bribe a young volunteer to bring her weekly updates on the new child who had been placed in the orphanage a few months ago.

So for the next few years, Prajakta made do with these updates, and photographs surreptitiously taken by the volunteer in exchange for payment. These kept her going.

That is, until the volunteer told her that her son had been adopted.

PRAJAKTA

I've only ever wanted what was best for my child.

If I didn't, would I have given him up?

But that doesn't mean I can't long for him, does it?

You will understand what I mean, Officer Gaekwad, when you have your own.

Yes, I did find out the names and address of the people who had adopted my son. I followed his trail to Mumbai.

I saw that they were wealthy people. I was glad. My son would have a good life.

He would grow up in luxury. Be treated like royalty.

That was enough for me.

But he was so close by. Would it really be so wrong for me to be close to him?

He was not mine anymore. I knew that.

He was no longer Alok Kolte. He was Anush Venkataraman. He belonged to Vishnu and Lalitha Venkataraman.

But how could I erase my child from my body? From my being?

Could I not just be close to him? I just wanted to be close to him.

So I used to walk past their apartment complex several times a day. It's a gated community of wealthy people; I could not find a way in easily. It took me a while before I managed to befriend the security guards of the complex.

I did what I needed to do to get them to put in a word for me.

Wealthy people, I have learnt, are usually unable to take care of themselves. Or their children. I got lucky when Nupur Balachandran interviewed and hired me as a part-time cook. I worked there for two years.

In the evenings, I would watch from Nupur madam's window as Lalitha went on her evening stroll, with my baby in her arms.

I knew I had to find a way to get employed at their residence. To be close to my baby. I just did not know how to do it.

But God is good. He would never want a child to be separated from his mother. One day, I overheard Nupur madam and Rashi madam discussing how Lalitha was having trouble finding a good nanny for my Alok.

One day, while Nupur madam was in the bathroom, I managed to mention to Rashi madam how I needed full-time work to make more money. My parents are ill, I told her. I'll do anything – cook, clean, take care of children.

I'm good with children, I told her. You've seen me with Nupur madam's daughter.

It worked. Rashi madam recommended me to Lalitha. Before I knew it, I had been summoned for an interview at the Venkataraman house.

I will never forget that moment when Alok came running towards me. He had grown so big! He looked so much like his father! Do you know what it feels like to be hugged for the first time by your own child, Officer? One day, you will. I pray that you will.

Everything changed after that. It was everything I had imagined I would want – being close to my child, holding him, feeding him. Everything I missed out on in the first years of his life.

As a bonus, I would also be able to watch him grow up in comfort, loved by the people he called his parents. So what if he could never know who I was? A mother wants what is best for her child.

But then, as he grew older, I watched Vishnu Venkataraman's cruelty grow. Both towards my son, and towards his own wife.

The man was vile.

I promise you, I did my best to understand. The man is ill, I told myself. He cannot beat the cancer forever.

But the old brute refused to give up. He lived, and he lived, and he lived.

And, with every passing year, he tortured my son more and more. Was I just supposed to sit and watch?

Initially, I did. I watched, quietly, my heart breaking and my whole body seething, as he shamed Alok day in and day out for his dyslexia. I watched as he abused his wife, and broke my son's self-confidence. I watched, helpless, as he kicked my son out of the house. I even stayed silent over the next few years, when I could not even see Alok, simply because Vishnu would not allow it.

But I have a breaking point too.

And the last straw was when, after the first wave, Alok visited us. That wretch Vishnu, instead of making him feel welcome, chased him out again.

And then told Lalitha that he would write Alok out of his will.

He did not know that I heard. Neither did Lalitha. Neither of them even noticed that I was there in the room. They barely noticed me otherwise, anyway. The help is always invisible.

But I heard him.

There was no way I was going to allow him to ruin my son's life – the son's whose responsibility *he* had vowed to take, the bastard!

I knew the man was sick. His post-Covid test results showed that his uric acid levels were through the roof. And then, of course, there was the cancer.

If only he could catch the virus once again, just once ... I was sure that would be too much for his wasted body to take.

The man deserved to die.

And so, when the Delta virus hit, I decided to try something.

Since Alok's departure, I was put in charge of Vishnu's care. So I began to order groceries and food from outside, and then, without sanitizing the packages or my hands, attend to the old man.

I would touch his face, clean his mouth, put on his mask … all with unsanitized hands.

Nobody had to know. Nobody could know. Especially not Lalitha. She was wasting away anyway, pining for Alok. Pining for my son.

I was aware I could fall sick too. I could die.

I did not care. If I died, I would be dying trying to do right by my son.

But God is good. Nothing happened to me.

Vishnu, however, caught the Delta virus.

And it hit him *hard*.

I remember the night he was hospitalized. He was delirious. It was wonderful to watch.

When Vishnu died, it felt like a victory like no other.

I had done right by my child. His tormentor was gone.

I remember calling my son to inform him about Vishnu's hospitalization. He had a right to know. I had to pretend to be shaken up.

I also remember Alok hanging up on me just when I was asking him if he was alright.

That hurt.

I did not like it.

He didn't even ask me if I was okay. All he said to me was, "Take care of Amma."

Only Amma. No Tai.

It also really hurt me when he tore himself out of my embrace and ran to Lalitha, the day he visited the house for the first time after the first wave.

I remember the feeling of holding him in my arms again. My baby boy, grown so big. My boy, whom I had not seen in a year.

I cried when I held him. He cried too, of course. He was happy to see me.

So why did he have to rip away from me to go to Lalitha? Does Tai not matter to him?

Do you know how much it hurts when your child pulls away from you, Officer Gaekwad? Do you think you will ever find out?

I pray you never do.

I pray you never find out how I felt that day when my son turned on me.

I had saved him and Lalitha from that man. I had stopped him from disowning Alok. He would never be able to harm my boy again. I did that! I did that for him!

But Alok? He only thanked his Amma for standing up to his father for him. What about Tai? Did Tai not stand up for him?

All he could see was how unwell Lalitha looked. His Amma. Always his Amma!

He accused me, mid-meal, of not taking care of his Amma. What would he have done if he knew everything I had already done for him and his Amma?

If he knew, would he have said what he said after that?

If he knew, would he have said he wanted me to leave?

Do you know how that feels? To be threatened with eviction by your own son?

After everything I have done for him?

After all that I have gone through for Alok – working for meagre pay in a factory, depending on the pity and largesse of others to just get news of him, following him all the way to a big city, allowing those security guards to do unspeakable things to me just to get a job recommendation, waiting patiently for years to finally be able to hold my son – he wanted to throw me out?

For *Lalitha*? The woman who could not even manage the child on her own till I came along?

Why would I want this woman to remain in my son's life? Isn't it only natural that I would want her gone?

What would you do, if you were in my place?

I did what I had to do. Lalitha had to go.

She is a good woman. Nothing like her brute of a husband. I did not want to hurt her.

I just wanted her to go. Painlessly. I wanted to make it easy for her.

It was easy enough for me, too. Lalitha was already frail; her years with Vishnu had not been kind on her, either mentally or physically.

She just needed slow, gradual nudges. Something to slow her down, help her sleep.

It's easy enough to help someone like that when you are in charge of their food and drink.

That tea you yanked out of my hands the day you barged into our house? I'd been infusing certain … herbs into it.

Every day, for a few weeks. It was in her food as well. Only hers, mind you. Not Alok's. But of course, you already know that. You've had everything searched and tested.

I promise you, I was only trying to help my son.

He deserved a mother who could be there for him, no matter what.

No matter what.

I am sorry I failed. I did my best.

Where is Alok, Officer Gaekwad? May I speak to him once? Please?

I just want to tell him that Tai loves him.

That his mother loves him.

ACKNOWLEDGEMENTS

In the life of a storyteller, ideas are paramount. And, as all my fellow storytellers will agree, inspiration can strike us anywhere, at any time, and under any conditions. This, then, begs the question: What do we do with all these ideas? How do we bring them all to life?

How do we tell all these stories?

It has been my dream for years to find the right voice to tell the stories here in The Silent Matter. To put pen to paper, and embrace this phase of a storyteller's journey.

And I could not have done it without the people who helped me realise my dream of writing my own stories. To them, I shall be eternally grateful.

Thank you, Nayantara Mazumder, for crafting the stories so perfectly. I am eternally grateful to you.

Thank you, Avik Chatterjee, for making me a storyteller.

Thank you, Harshita Deshpande, for constantly inspiring me in whatever I do, and for the name of my book.

Thank you, Anjan Chatterjee, for being there as a silent supporter.

Thank you, Avyan Deshpande, for defining joy and laughter for me, in your own, new, way.

Thank you, Aditya Deshpande, for always listening to my stories with so much patience

Thank you, Rhea Chatterjee, for always giving me your unconditional support.

Thank you, Sumit Dasgupta, for being a true friend. Without you, this book would not have happened.

Thank you, Ramona Sen, for making sure that this book is sent out into the universe. It could not be more perfect.

Thank you, Urvashi Thakkad, my dearest friend, for always being there for me unconditionally.

Thank you, Anima Aurora, for your constant support and encouragement.

Thank you, Aarti Bajaj, for making me feel alive again.

And finally, thank you, Maa, for being my endless source of strength and courage.